Foreign Constellations

Foreign Constellations

—THE FANTASTIC WORLDS OF—

John Brunner

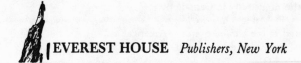 EVEREST HOUSE *Publishers, New York*

Library of Congress Cataloging in Publication Data:
Brunner, John, 1934-
  Foreign constellations.
  CONTENTS: The Berendt conversion.—The easy way out.—Out of
mindshot.—Pond water. [etc.]
  1. Science fiction, English. I. Title.
PZ4.B89Gal   1980 [PR6052.R8]   823'914   79-92183
ISBN: 0-89696-094-3

Contents

Acknowledgments

The Berendt Conversion first appeared in *Ramparts,* July 1975, Copyright © 1975 by Noah's Ark Inc., and was included in *Fireweed* #9, June 1977.

The Easy Way Out first appeared in *If,* June 1971, Copyright © 1971 by UPD Publishing Corp., and was included in *Best Science Fiction for 1972,* edited by Frederick Pohl (Ace Books).

Out of Mindshot first appeared in *Galaxy,* June 1970, Copyright © 1970 by Universal Publishing and Distributing Corp., and was included in *The Best from Galaxy, Volume 1* (Award Books).

Pond Water first appeared in *The Farthest Reaches,* edited by Joseph Elder (Trident Press), Copyright © 1968 by Joseph Elder

The Protocols of the Elders of Britain first appeared in *Stopwatch,* edited by George Hay (New English Library), Copyright © 1974 by John Brunner, and was included in *The 1976 Annual World's Best SF,* edited by Donald A. Wollheim (DAW Books).

The Suicide of Man first appeared in *Isaac Asimov's Science Fiction Magazine,* July-August 1978, Copyright © 1978 by Davis Publications.

The Taste of the Dish and the Savour of the Day first appeared in *The Magazine of Fantasy & Science Fiction,* August 1977, Copyright © 1977 by Mercury Press Inc., and was included in *The 1978 Annual World's Best SF,* edited by Donald A. Wollheim (DAW Books).

What Friends Are For first appeared in *Fellowship of the Stars,* edited by Terry Carr (Simon & Schuster), Copyright © 1974 by Terry Carr, and was included in *Best Science Fiction Stories of the Year #4,* edited by Lester Del Rey (E.P. Dutton).

Foreign Constellations

The Berendt Conversion

*U*nder the cloud–dark sky that promised rain by sunset: the noise of an approaching engine. Heads were turned. The soup–tanker was of course what everybody was looking forward to, but it couldn't possibly be here for at least another hour and would be later still if the crew had to beat off an attempted hijack. Anyhow, what was coming was a helicopter and those had been reserved since spring for moving people, not goods.

It was a bad time for the unexpected. Five wars were in progress over food.

Therefore soldiers' knuckles paled on the hands that held their guns. Many of them had seen service during hunger riots last year and the year before. Workers trudging down from the hills with burdens of miscellaneous vegetation reflexively glanced around in search of cover. In the supermarket car-park the non-working refugees reacted also, bar the handful who were too weak. But those were mostly children. This operation had an admirable record. Some days nobody died here at all.

The youngest of the five policemen whose job it was to keep order among the inhabitants of the car park was proud of his contribution to this exceptional achievement. Before permitting himself to look up he took time to survey his charges. Most were sheltered by abandoned cars and delivery trucks; even the least fortunate were protected from wind and rain, if not from cold, by tents improvised out of plastic sheet and aluminium pipe. Now and then someone in a tent noticed that someone in a more substantial home was weakening and took advantage of the police's backs being turned to kick out the luckier neighbours. Once there had been an epidemic of such attacks and for a week more fatalities were due to murder than to hunger.

Not presently, however. And the young policeman had no

opinion, private or public, concerning the latrine rumour which claimed that the protein content of the soup had been cut to increase fatigue and forestall another similar outbreak.

As soon as they realised the chopper was neither shooting nor being shot at, the refugees and workers slumped back in time to where they had been a moment earlier: the latter because payout was as distant as usual, the former—it could be read in their hostile eyes—because they feared more mouths were being brought, more empty bellies.

The soldiers would have done likewise but that the sergeant in charge of the assessment detail ordered them to stand to. The earliest-returning of the workers were coming up to the perimeter gate with their day's forages, demanding to be let pass along the barbed wire corridor into the supermarket, that horrible echoing cavern of a place where the only light came from holes blasted in the walls and meshed over against thieves, or cold refugees jealous that the soldiers and police should sleep under such solid cover.

The young policeman had often wondered what it was like to run that gauntlet at the end of a hard day: to face the scales, then the sonic testers employed to determine how much usable greenery, how much woody matter, and how much dirt and gravel made up the weight of each bag and basket, then let his hand be stamped with a code indicating what food he was to be allotted when the tanker pulled in with its loaf-nets sagging on either side.

Funny ... As the summer wore to its end more and more of the workers seemed to be losing touch with reality, trying to deceive the assessors by hiding pebbles among the leaves and roots they could legitimately gain credit for, even though they must surely by now be aware that all such trickery was certain to be found out. Yesterday indeed a man who should have known better, being father of five children including a recent baby, had been fool enough to alter the *1* stamped on his hand to a *4* and in accordance with regulations had been refused any food at all. It wasn't fair on the kids for him to have done that.

His eyes strayed to the hillside. To left, to right and also at his back, the slopes were littered with what had been handsome expensive homes before the ghetto-ghouls began their rampage through this valley. He tried to picture it as it had been five years earlier; failed, because as a kid he had never lived in nor even visited such a wealthy suburb; then tried not to visualise it as it inevitably would be after the winter and failed again. But for the frequent rain this land would already be shedding dust this fall as once it had shed leaves.

The helicopter settled on the patch where the soup-tanker ordinarily drew up, the most defensible spot. Alerted by radio, the commanding colonel and his adjutant were on hand. An armed private with the professionally paranoid air of a bodyguard jumped out, only condescending to salute after he had swept the vicinity with his suspicious gaze. Then an *important* passenger climbed down, encumbered with a bulging paunch, and shook the colonel's hand and marched off with him to the supermarket.

Among the refugees there had grown up a ritual to be performed on catching sight of anybody fat. Behind the wire a defiant old man demonstrated it, being himself as scrawny as a beanpole; he spat on the ground, trod on the spittle, turned his back with an over-shoulder scowl. To this the young policeman was directed to reply with a gesture towards his gun and a threatening glare, rehearsed again and again to render it maximally convincing and save the ammunition that would be wasted were he to have to shoot.

But the landing of the chopper had saved him from—from something. He had been on the edge of—of—of . . . It wouldn't come clear. He could, though, sense it would have been disastrous. (Maybe he himself would in a fit of craziness have spat on seeing how fat the visitor was?)

He did not even drop his hand to his holster. He simply stood and shivered, more from the narrowness of his escape from—from whatever it was he *had* escaped, than from the chill that harbingered the rain.

Who was this person, anyhow, who rated a slow, expensive, wasteful mode of transport like a chopper in times of planetary dearth? The machine's pilot, a lean man with a close-trimmed dark beard, had got out and stood a few feet away, stretching himself limb by limb as he looked the scene over. The young policeman attempted to utter a greeting, pose a question ... and abruptly couldn't. His mouth was watering incredibly. He had caught a scent so indescribably delicious it dizzied him. It awoke hunger that seemed to cry out from his very cells.

Hideously embarrassed, he gulped and gulped, hoping the bearded man would not notice. Seemingly he was more interested in the workers returning with their loads of greenstuff and the armed men lined up to receive them.

After a few moments he said, "Get much trouble with thieves, do you?"

The salivation was coming under control. (What *could* have triggered it?) "Not twice," the policeman managed to quote.

The pilot glanced at him as though surprised. "Hmm! It's long since I heard *that* crack! Must have been when the cows went on their involuntary seven-year diet ... Still, I guess granary guards are much alike wherever and whenever."

The policeman let that pass without bothering about its meaning. Now that he could speak normally again, he preferred to put the question he had originally intended about the passenger.

"Government food chemist," the pilot answered.

The policeman essayed a joke. "Looks as though he tests his products on himself, doesn't it?"

A merely polite smile. "If you knew him you couldn't picture him being his own guinea pig ... Oh–oh. Here it comes!"

Like stabbing needles the first drops of rain. In the car-park the refugees ducked under cover; workers lining up to be shepherded into the supermarket made what use they could of their bundled twigs and leaves.

"Inside, quickly!"

The policeman started. The pilot had scrambled back into his seat; now he was patting the place next to him, which had been occupied by the bodyguard. There were two more seats in back. One, the passenger's, was empty. In the other dozed a top sergeant, a man heavy-set without being fat, on whom the refugees would not have expended spittle, with great pouches under his eyes and sagging empty jowls that testified to his having lost much poundage since—since whenever. He snored occasionally.

"Come on!" the pilot urged. "The rain's doing half your work for you, isn't it?"

True, true. It dampened spirits as it wet the ground. He climbed three wide-spaced rungs and sat, pulling the door to behind him. At once his mouth flooded again. The same scent was in the air, far stronger.

"It's no fit way for a human being to end the day's work," the pilot muttered. He was staring as the workers formed a tidy line between the spikes of barbed wire and of bayonets. "To sweat from dawn to dusk, creep homeward folded double by your load, be told there's too much dirt and grit in it, half rations for your family tonight ... *And* it's making more desert when we need less."

The policeman had heard that sort of talk before. But when people were starving by the tens of millions it was no time for fancy fits of conscience. Just so long as they were kept alive.

"You got a patch of dirt on your face," the pilot said after a pause. "Right cheekbone."

The policeman almost raised his hand to rub before he remembered. "Oh, that. No, it isn't dirt. I guess I bruised it somehow."

"Ah–hah?" The pilot scrutinised him. "Bruise easily, do you? Yes? Do your joints hurt?"

"Sometimes. Seems to be a thing going around."

"Be damned," the pilot said softly. "I knew the refugees were getting it, but I thought at least the guards ... Here, boy." He reached under the instrument panel and produced a lunchbox previously hidden in shadow. The instant he opened it the delicious scent became unbearable.

"Boy?" the policeman bridled.

"Hell, if you're old enough to vote I'll personally eat the shit you've passed since your birthday...." Taking from the box something brown and white, something pink, something round and red. Also a knife.

"Should give you an orange or a lemon," the pilot said musingly. "Don't have any by me, though.... What's 'going around', as you call it, is something we've known the cure for since about the eighteenth century—scurvy. I recall at Alexandria it made the soldiers so listless they paid no attention when the enemy approached. Bad stuff. Here, eat this. Best be quick and not let any of the refugees see you with it." He held out a swiftly-fashioned sandwich of bread and ham, and also a tomato.

"Are they real?" the young policeman breathed.

"I should live so long and grow so rich! Hell, no. These are berendtised."

"All made out of—of...?" With a gesture at the workers' forage.

"Sure, but don't be put off. It's not rat-meat I'm giving you. That's officer-grade food, four hundred fifty bucks' worth of power to every pound. You won't taste the same again in a hurry ... Mark you, when there's nothing else even rat-meat can be tasty."

Taking the sandwich gingerly the policeman said, "I never got that far down. Seen plenty that did, of course. Uh—where were you reduced to rats?"

"Oh, there's nothing very special about rats. After the cats and dogs are all gone ... In Paris, though: that was something else. We had some very strange meats when we cleared out the Zoo—elephant, giraffe, even python ... Say, eat up, will you, instead of staring? It's not poisoned!"

The policeman opened his mouth and crammed it in, trying to savour each crumb and morsel, failing because his hunger was so deep, so keen.

"Oh, God," he said at length, and ran his tongue hopefully around his lips to trap a last elusive drop of tomato juice. In back, the sleeping sergeant shifted but didn't open his eyes.

The pilot closed the lunchbox and carefully put it away. There was a little silence, but for the sound of rain. At last the policeman said, "I heard a story about Berendt. Is it true he killed himself by jumping into his own food-converter?"

"It's true he killed himself. Whether he did it in that precise way is just about impossible to find out. They prefer people not to know they killed him."

"What? You just said he killed himself and now—"

"Did you never wonder what decided him?"

"Ah . . . Well, sure. It seems kind of odd he did it just when he'd succeeded in his life's ambition, right?"

"Ambition," the pilot repeated thoughtfully. "Obsession may have been more like it. The story goes he never talked or thought about anything except his plan to save the world from famine."

"What—what drove him, do you think?"

"Heaven knows. Some people say his father had been eaten. Things like that did happen. It was a vicious winter. Of course it was just a Little Hunger, and at that it was in wartime. The Big Hunger hadn't more than started."

"Where was that?"

"Leningrad."

There was another pause. Now dusk and denser rain had almost veiled the late-returning workers. The soldiers, as wet and cold as their charges, were beginning to raise their voices and threaten to cuff with gun-butts.

"For whatever reason," the pilot resumed unexpectedly, "Yakov Berendt made the food converter his personal crusade. He had no scientific talent, so the first thing he had to do was

make a fortune so he could hire top chemists and engineers and
dietitians. It cost every penny he had just to build one pilot
model. But when he had that, he had proof it could be done. He
was able to borrow. Altogether he borrowed over twenty million. Produced the machine he'd always dreamed of. Drop in
any kind of vegetation, even the poisonous kind, even the useless
kind like straw and twigs, fit the right master-tape, and out
would come good nourishing food. How could there be any
more starvation when there was one of his machines in every
village?"

"But there isn't," the policeman said, settling back comfort-
ably in his seat and folding his hands on his stomach. It was
amazing how full and sleepy that one sandwich had made him.

"Right. There isn't. With the Big Hunger looming larger by
the day, the people who had loaned him the money to develop
the converter branded him a crank and a lunatic and had him
voted off his own company's board. Once they were in control
they made sure the price of a Berendt converter was the highest
the market could bear. No, there are not converters in every village. But there are in every smart restaurant and hotel. And
some private homes, come to that. This guy I'm ferrying
around: he has one." The pilot scowled into the gathering dark.

"But in any case," he added, "he was completely wrong to
think his machine could save us."

"How's that again?" The policeman's eyes threatened to drift
shut; he forced the lids apart and forced himself to concentrate
on what the pilot was saying.

"Proof is all about us. Like I said, this project and those like it
are making more desert when we need less. There's nothing
wonderful about being a villager, you know—what reason is
there to think peasants would behave any differently from
townsfolk? Just as your rich family in the big city buys dirt-
cheap rubbish for the converter and puts on an expensive
tape and eats the *haute cuisine,* so villagers would have been content to chuck in leaves and grass and the hell with actually
planting anything. Who wants to break his back for corn and

cabbages? Food from the converter is better than most of what you get from the ground; they choose only the very finest models to make up tapes from. Why, they've got to the stage now where they can duplicate vintage wines. The experts say they're more consistent than the original."

"I wouldn't know," the policeman muttered. "Never tasted wine . . . Say, you didn't finish telling me why Berendt committed suicide."

"It could have been because of what his partners planned to do with the converter; could equally have been because he suddenly realised his idea was stupid from the start. By the time he got the machine working it was already far too late. We were set for our population crash, one of the classic two-thirds degree. No point in arguing with laws of nature."

"Now wait a minute. Nature doesn't always rule us. We've changed the face of nature for a start. First time we ploughed a field, wasn't that going against nature?"

"If it was, it likely didn't work. Things like that succeed when you're working with nature, not against. Heard the news today?"

"Been on duty since dawn. No."

"There's civil war in Brazil. The people who accepted land grants in rain-forest areas and cleared them without realising that when you expose the ground it turns to a rock-hard crust which won't grow anything: they lost patience and took out after the bastards who sold them this bill of goods. A grenade killed the provincial governor and his senior aide last night; today the country's under martial law." The pilot stabbed the air with his forefinger. "What happened to those Brazilian farms: that's what I mean when I talk about going against nature. You have to coax her, never drive her. And we're still animals for all our cleverness. Animals that outstrip their food supply suffer a population crash, and the rate is almost always two out of three. Rabbits. Lemmings. All kinds of animals. And us. And it's such a horrible state to be reduced to . . . I remember in India, where they had fourteen famines in ninety years.

As the famine increased, men abandoned towns and villages and wandered helplessly. It was easy to recognise their condition: eyes sunk deep in the head; lips pale and covered with slime; the skin hard, with the bones showing through; the belly nothing but a pouch hanging down empty; knuckles and knee-caps showing prominently. One would cry and howl for hunger, while another lay on the ground dying in misery. Wherever you went, you saw nothing but corpses."

The policeman shivered, though the cabin was snug and wind-tight.

"And it was bad in Skibbereen, too. That's Ireland. One village called South Reen seemed to be deserted when we went there with supplies of bread. So we looked in some of the houses—hovels, really. In the first, six famished and ghastly skeletons, to all appearances dead, were huddled in a corner on some filthy straw, their sole covering what seemed a ragged horse-cloth, and their wretched legs hanging about naked above the knees. I approached with horror, and found by a low moaning they were alive. They were in fever—four children, a woman, and what had once been a man . . .

"In another case my clothes were nearly torn off in my endeavours to escape from a throng of pestilence around, when my neck-cloth was seized from behind by a grip which compelled me to turn. I found myself grasped by a woman with an infant just born in her arms, and the remains of a filthy sack across her loins—the sole covering of herself and babe. The same morning the police opened a house on the adjoining lands which was observed shut for many days, and two frozen corpses were found lying upon the mud floor, half devoured by the rats . . .

"A mother, herself in fever, was seen the same day to drag out the corpse of her child, a girl of about twelve, perfectly naked, and leave it half covered with stones. In another house within 500 yards of the cavalry station at Skibbereen the dispensary doctor found seven wretches lying, unable to move, under the same cloak—one had been dead many hours, but the others were unable to move themselves or the corpse."

"Well, if it's really a law of nature . . ." the policeman said, staring appalled at the pilot's calm face.

"Oh, I believe in the law all right. It doesn't say the two-thirds we're going to lose can't be the *right* two-thirds." He gave a harsh laugh. "Starting with people who starve others out of megalomania and greed. They'd be *no* loss. This guy, this food chemist I'm nursemaiding: he's like that. Reminds me a lot of John of Leyden. Real name was Bockelson but he preferred the short form. More like a king's name, I guess.

"And that was how he saw himself. Somehow he conned a gang of people in Münster into setting up a fantasy kingdom with him and his sidekicks at the top. Well, the Empire wasn't going to put up with that, so they set siege to the place and starved the defenders out. The self-styled king requisitioned all the food in the city and had all the horses killed. At all times the royal court ate well and had sufficient stocks of meat, corn, wine and beer for half a year. The rest were not so lucky. Every animal—dog, cat, mouse, rat, hedgehog—was killed and eaten and people began to consume grass and moss, old shoes and the whitewash on the walls, the bodies of the dead."

"Whitewash?" the policeman said incredulously.

"Oh, sure. People have been known to eat dirt; haven't you seen them? Even short of that, people put some funny things in their bellies. I remember on Guernsey they drank stuff made from parsnips and fruit leaves instead of tea. Smoked some peculiar things too. Made cigarettes out of dried potato peel—bramble leaves—rose-petals . . . even plain grass. Anything to stave off the pangs. Coming back from Moscow we boiled our boots and the leather harness left over after we'd eaten the horses, brewed something warm with the illusion of nourishment."

"I heard about people boiling boots," the policeman said. "Thought it was a joke."

"Not so funny when it happens to you," said the pilot. "Like I say, we'd finished the horses. Deprived of fodder and constantly exposed, they died in great numbers. Often men did not wait until the horses had fallen to devour them . . . A stray horse was instantly killed and dismembered almost living: unlucky animal who moved a few steps away from his master . . . A lot of fights got started over who was to have what bit."

Cold—unspeakable terrible cold—seemed to reach into the chopper. It was so completely numbing, one could not even shiver.

Eventually the policeman was able to say, "I get the feeling we here are—well, you'd have to call us lucky, I guess."

"Sure. You're very lucky. Only thing apt to delay your daily rations is a bunch of people half out of their minds and armed with shotguns they have no more shells for. While in Africa . . . You said you didn't hear the news today?"

"Not yet."

"Well, they had to ground the UN relief flights. Seems Zaïre got paranoid. Decided they aren't getting enough relief and all their neighbours are getting so much they're planning to trade it to Europe and buy arms in order to invade. So they dusted off their ground-to-air missiles—they got these good ones made in Switzerland—and started shooting down the UN planes. Pilots won't fly the missions any more, and do you blame 'em?"

"That's terrible!"

"Not so much terrible as typical. In L.A., you know, they'd put up a rick of oranges and apples, put gasoline over it and set fire to them. Vegetables were being destroyed and everything. To keep the price up. But there were great queues of guys in soup lines. Nobody had a dime." The pilot shook his head. "It's the 'I-don't-want-it-you-can't-have-it' syndrome. See it all the time in spoiled kids."

"I guess maybe it's as well Berendt did away with himself," the policeman said. "Whether he jumped into his converter or not. If he was alive he'd be the world's most disappointed man."

He hesitated. "Funny, you know. Talking to you makes me think about him as a person for the first time. Always before I've had this impression of him as—well, close to a saint. Spent his whole life for the sake of others and it isn't his fault his dream never came true."

From the back of the cabin, a snorting noise. They looked behind and found the sergeant was awake.

"I've been listening to you, Jacobson," he said, pushing his blocky torso upright. "Spinning these crazy lies to someone who's no more than a kid—it's disgusting. Hear me? What you said about Ireland: it's not true. I got family in Ireland and they just wrote me and said yoù can buy butter without a ration card. Natural butter! Can't do that here, can you? Does that sound like starvation?" Aside to the policeman. "And I just saw this TV report about Paris, too. And they are *not* burning food in L.A.—lies, all of it!"

The pilot winked sidelong at the policeman, who was bewildered.

"As for Berendt!" The sergeant leaned forward, hands on the back of the pilot's seat and clenching tight as though he would rather have gripped the other's throat. "Berendt did *not* jump into his own machine and there is *not* a little of him in everything that comes out of a converter and it's a load of blasphemous nonsense. I wish you weren't civilian personnel—I'd like to sort you out the way you deserve."

With a final glare he slumped back and concluded, "Out with you, boy. You've had enough of this bastard's yarn-spinning."

Confused, the policeman opened the door to the rain and jumped down. Approaching were a group of men under an umbrella: the food chemist, an escorting officer and the bodyguard.

"They're coming back!" he called to the pilot, who also clambered down.

And said very softly, almost without moving his lips but contriving to make himself heard perfectly: "So maybe Yakov Berendt didn't wind up in a food-converter. But I'll tell you who did. The guy I used to fly around before this one. And soon's I get the chance he'll be the next." With ever so slight an inclination of the head. "Like I said, we need to make sure it's the right two-thirds of mankind we dispose of. Thanks to Berendt we have the means to make them useful for a change. Tell people that. Tell people you can trust."

He clapped the younger man on the shoulder, then went on loudly, "Did everything go off all right, sir?"

"Perfectly, thank you, Joseph," said the important passenger. "Though it took longer than I expected. I hope you weren't too bored."

"Not at all, sir," said the pilot. "Not at all." And made to help the fat man up the ladder.

For several minutes after the chopper had taken off the policeman was in a kind of daze. Extraordinary images kept flashing through his mind: some ludicrous, like a pan full of boots being boiled, and others ghastly, like an emaciated child licking a whitewashed wall.

And that parting remark. To be taken seriously? Surely it must be some sort of sick joke!

He was recalled to the present by the roaring noise of the soup-tanker as it ground to a halt among cheers from refugees and soldiers alike. It was a tradition to signal its arrival in that fashion. Automatically the young policeman started to join in.

And checked.

He looked at the bulky tanker with the loaf-nets dangling from it, thought of the grass and leaves and twigs and roots it would carry in those nets when it left here and returned to its base in the nearest city.

Thought of what would happen to that greenstuff. Thought of tomato juice on his chin, bread, ham ... and then of the greyish quarter-loaf he would receive at supper, gritty in texture, under its sour crust more hole than crumb. That, and a bowl of the invariable watery broth in which floated a few anonymous vegetables. It was a common game to make bets on their identity. There was never meat, of course. It cost too much.

After a while he started wondering whom he could trust enough to tell about the Berendt conversion.

AFTERWORD

Some of Joseph the son of Jacob's reminiscences should instantly be recognisable, above all the reference to the years of the ill-favoured kine. However, a few are likely to leave the reader in the infuriating state, "I'm sure I know where that comes from, but . . . !"

So here are the sources.

The description of scurvy among the soldiers at Alexandria is from Larrey's memoirs; he was Surgeon-General to Napoleon. The Paris Zoo was used to supplement the rations of the besieged during the Franco–Prussian War. (They ate some even odder things than python.) Cannibalism at Leningrad is a recurrent rumour, recurrently denied.

The civil war in Brazil hasn't happened yet; however, the land those poor devils are trying to farm was seen in a British TV documentary a few years ago. The description of the Indian famine is from the memoirs of a Dutch merchant called Van Twist, who was there in 1630–31. (The fourteen famines were from 1660 to 1750.) The man who took bread to the village of South Reen was a local justice of the peace; this is from a letter he wrote to the Duke of Wellington which W. O. O'Brien quoted in his book *The Great Famine*.

Authority for the diet of the subjects of John of Leyden can be found in Norman Cohn's *The Pursuit of the Millennium*. The comment about what people can be driven to put in their bellies paraphrases a remark in *The Oxford Book of Food Plants*; the authors say, "Nor is it possible to include all those plants (though some are mentioned) which men will try to eat in the desperation of famine." The specific examples given, and the ersatz cigarettes, are from the recollection of people who lived in Guernsey under Nazi occupation, 1940–45, and I found them in Comer Clarke's *England Under Hitler*.

The horses eaten almost before their death are from Larrey again. The burning of fruit to keep the price up is quoted verbatim from *Hard Times* by Studs Terkel. And except that in those days they were using artillery instead of guided missiles, the shooting-down of UN relief planes could well refer to the Nigeria-Biafra war.

—JKHB

The Easy Way Out

No human being had any right to survive the crash of the Pennyroyal: tumbling insanely out of space through air that bit blazing chunks from its hull, down a thirty-mile sandslope sown with rocks, and ultimately wrong end first into a vast dune which absorbed it like a bullet ricocheting into the bank around a rifle range.

By a minor miracle the sand put out the fires on board. There had been a lot of those.

After that nothing happened for a long time.

I'm alive.

The thought floated sluggishly into Pavel Williamson's mind. He hated it. He was half-buried in something dense and yielding, and he was almost suffocated by choking fumes. Moreover he had been tumbled around and around in total blackness until he was sick with giddiness. His head ached foully, there was a taste of blood in his mouth, he seemed to be one vast bruise from the waist down, and there was a sharp pain in his right ankle.

Taken by themselves, those minor injuries were not sufficient reason for preferring not to be alive. But there was another, more important reason. As the ship's medical officer, not concerned with matters of navigation, he had no precise idea where the *Pennyroyal* had been when a vast explosion shook it like a hammer blow, but he was absolutely certain that the planet they had crashed on was not the one they were bound for, a safe Earth-type world.

Therefore these fumes which were swirling about him might all too easily not be fumes at all, but the planet's unbreathable atmosphere. In which case the best—the only—sane course open to him was to compose himself and wait for merciful extinction.

27

He was not a professional spaceman, just a young doctor who had signed on with a succession of spacelines in order to see a little of the inhabited galaxy before settling down on a world which suited him, but he had been impressed by the autohypnotic formulae some spacemen used in emergencies like this one. Closing his eyes—not that they had shown him anything when they were open, because it was absolutely dark in here—he began to recite one in his head.

And stopped.

A banging noise!

Some part of the wreckage settling? Something falling on a resonant steel floor? Most likely—

But it wasn't! He jerked, and cursed his injured ankle which responded with another arrow of pain. No, the bangs had been too regular—and there they came again: one–two–three, pause, one–two–three, pause. Like a man hitting a bulkhead with a fist, or some hard object.

It dawned on him that someone else must be alive nearby, and that if someone else had survived the crash, it might not have been as bad as he'd assumed, and together he and some helpers might rig some sort of beacon to help a search party locate the wreck.

And if the fumes were fumes, not bad air, then they might have come down on—

He fumbled frantically among the mass of soft stuff he was almost over ears in, wondering what it was, and recognized it in moments. Furs! He'd known the *Pennyroyal* had a cargo of furs on board—it had been part of his duties when they were loaded to check them for parasites and disease germs—and he had seen them being stowed in a compartment adjacent to his surgery. Fur traders often paid the extra cost of shipping their wares on a liner instead of a freighter; now and then, a sale to one of the wealthier passengers not only wiped out the difference in charges but actually made a profit. Presumably the reason they were out of their bales was that they'd been on display when the explosion occurred. And he himself—he worked it out because the pattern of his bruises matched the theory—had been hurled through a weak spot in the bulkhead, flimsy to conserve weight, and landed against a wad of them thick enough to save his life.

Floundering, almost swimming, he began to force himself to the surface of the pile, and realized as he did so that his weight felt only a trifle less than Earth-normal. His spirits rose. The air around might then be breathable after all. The system they had been bound for was among the rare ones which boasted two oxygen-high planets: their destination, Carteret, and another which had not been colonized. This was the fringe of human space, and the original impulse which had carried the species so far so fast was waning. Conquering a brand-new world when there was another next door considerably warmer and more hospitable was not an attractive proposition.

In any case, "oxygen-high" was only a comparative term. If his guess were right, and they were on the next planet out from Carteret, the air would be of poor quality because the vegetation from the sea had as yet barely begun to invade the land; most of it was desert, either sandy or rocky and in both cases chilly. The shoreline plants put about two-thirds of Earth-normal oxygen into the air, and they were mutating rapidly and extending their terrain, so in a million years or so one could look forward to a marked improvement.

Hah!

For the time being, though, what counted was that conditions could be endured, if not enjoyed, on Quasimodo IV. He reminded himself that he must take things easy as he fought his way out of the furs—he couldn't recall offhand what the CO_2 count was in the air here, but he knew it was dangerously high. Indeed, the throbbing ache in his head was probably due to it rather than to the blow which had cut his eyebrow and sent a trail of blood down to the corner of his mouth.

Something hard and cool met his probing right hand. He recognized the shape: one of his medical instruments, a lung inspector. And next to it—

He withdrew his hand with an oath. Something wet and soft.

He preferred not to wonder about what it had been before the crash, and was glad of the darkness.

The triple banging came again, but weaker. There would be time enough to search for his equipment later, he decided, and continued his attempts to work free of the furs.

When eventually he found solid footing, he groped his way across a tilted floor, located what he had suspected—a rip in the bulkhead—and slithered through it, snagging his shirt on a projecting spike of hard plastic. Beyond, there was light. Not much, just a pale wash of daylight leaking through a gash in the hull, very yellow to his dark-adjusted vision. But it was daylight, and this was natural air he was breathing, contaminated with smoke from the crash, and there was gritty sand under his feet, all of which went to confirm his guess about arriving on Quasimodo IV.

He would have felt almost cheerful but that by this dim reflected sunlight he was able to see the ruin of his surgery. Everything had been spilled out from every cupboard, every drawer, every shelf, and he had to push confused piles of medical phials and instruments out of the way with his toes to find a path across the room. In two places the wall had split open, revealing the electronic veins and arteries of the ship, and something was dripping loudly somewhere.

But he would have to leave a proper investigation of the mess until he had located the other survivors.

Brackets around that plural "s."

It was like walking into a nightmare to turn along the crumpled corridor in the direction of the noise he'd heard. Everything was distorted, and although the little light which guided him came in only through cracks in the hull there were all too many such cracks and he saw more detail than he would have liked. At the extreme end of the passageway, in particular, there was something which looked loathsomely half-human, as though one were to make a doll from overripe bananas and hurl it at a wall: *splat!* Even as a trained medical man, he didn't as yet feel up to facing it.

Now he located the noise. It was coming from one of the nearest first-class passenger cabins, the door of which was stiff but still moving in its grooves. He slid it aside and found a young man lying in a bunk which had torn completely loose from its mountings. He had something in his limp hand, the object he had used to bang on the wall, Pavel presumed, but it appeared that while he was opening the door the man's strength had failed him, for he now lay still.

His heart sank. Of all the people aboard, he would have chosen this man last to be his companion after the crash: Andrew Solichuk, who had never tired of informing anyone and everyone how wealthy and influential his family was back on Earth and had complained endlessly about the food, the lack of comfort and amenities, the taste of the air, and the company he had to endure simply because he was on a grand tour of the commercial empire he was due to inherit and there was no luxury line serving the Quasimodo system, only the *Pennyroyal* and her sister ship the *Elecampane*.

But he was human, and alive. Pavel forced his professional reflexes to take over. He called Andrew's name, and elicited no reaction; the man appeared to have fainted. He checked his pulse and found it weak, but not failing; also his breathing was tolerably even. But when he pulled back the coverlet of the bunk he saw why Andrew had passed out. At the very least he must have suffered a compound fracture of the lower spine; quite probably he also had a broken pelvis, and there must certainly be internal injuries.

There was no trace of blood at his mouth, which indicated— though it did not prove—that his lungs were intact. But his left shoulder was dislocated, and there was a cut on his scalp which had soaked his pillow with blood.

Trivia like that he could take care of with water, any sterile dressing he could find in an untorn package, and his own strength. Otherwise, though, there was literally nothing he could do except make Andrew comfortable until help arrived. Taking a spine to bits and rebuilding it was a job for a modern hospital, and he half-doubted whether even the facilities on Carteret would be up to the task.

Since Andrew was currently unconscious, the best thing to do for the moment was to leave him that way while he determined whether any other survivors had lived through the crash, and sorted through the mess in his surgery to salvage what he could.

He crept very softly back into the corridor.

It took him only a few minutes to become convinced that there was no hope of any other survivor. On top of his other irritating habits, Andrew was ostentatiously "liberated from the tyranny of clocks." He invariably slept until late in the ship's artificial day, fourteen or fifteen hours, and then made merry until the small hours regardless of the people he inconvenienced, whether by his loud drunken laughter, his insistence on playing music at maximum volume, or the stamping dances he had learned on some planet or other earlier in his trip. In particular Hans, the ship's steward, hated him, because he felt he was entitled to human service despite the perfectly good automatics everyone else relied on, and during most of the voyage had kept Hans dancing attendance on him for so much of the "night" the poor man had to make do with three or four hours' sleep.

And it was this which had saved Andrew's miserable life. Everybody else had been up and about in the after part of the ship, and that was full of sand, poured in by the ton when the hull broke apart. There wasn't a chance in a million of recovering someone alive from that mass of grit and gravel. It was going to be tough unearthing from it food, water, and other essentials for their survival. Pavel suspected he might have to tear loose a hull-plate to use as a shovel.

It was a gloomy consolation that his guess about their location was being proved correct at every step he took. Despite the ache in his head, which was now growing almost intolerable, and the leaden heaviness of his limbs, when he had completed his survey of the reachable areas of the ship he postponed his return to the surgery for the sake of scrambling up one of the heaps of whitish sand and grit beside the cracks in the hull and peered out, having to steady himself by clinging tightly to the edges of the hole because the footing he had was so precarious.

Overhead, the sky was a uniform dark blue, close to indigo. The sun, slanting low in the sky, was small and very yellow. The air was cool, though not cold; perhaps the high proportion of unreduced CO_2 in it was enhancing the greenhouse effect and producing a disproportionately high daytime temperature. But on the other hand it was dry and harsh in his throat. They must be a long way from open water.

With a supreme effort he hoisted himself up far enough to look over the scarred and battered hull-plates in the direction away from the sun, and instantly realised how it had come about that the ship had not simply been smashed to fragments. There was a vast furrow in the sandy plain, dotted with boulders, on that side, and the level of the ground seemed to slant slightly upward, though the strain of holding himself on his arms was blurring his vision and it was difficult to make out details. Nonetheless, the pattern fitted: the glancing angle at which the ship had struck the ground must have been parallel to the slope, and instead of stopping dead (he wished he hadn't thought of that metaphor) it had gone skidding and grinding onwards for mile after mile. Until it had shed its initial velocity and piled into the dune.

Well, it was comforting to know he could still think, reason, solve puzzles. He let himself drop back into the heap of sand and headed wearily for the surgery.

Quasimodo IV, he thought. *Perhaps I'm the first human to see it from ground level in a hundred years.*

But there was nothing in the least exciting about that.

Almost the first thing he came on in the surgery which was intact enough to be of any use was a box of stimulant injectors, one out of a stock of perhaps forty or fifty which had been crushed into glass-prickly ruin. He tried to decide whether it was wise to give himself a shot, found he couldn't make his mind up, and did so.

At once his head cleared, and an artificial clarity informed his thoughts. New energy came to him, and rediscovered appetite. But as yet he had not located any food, and he was sure that when he did it would be after long burrowing into the sand dune. He repressed all thought of eating with a violent act of will, and went on hunting vigorously through the tangle of instruments and the stocks of drugs.

Within half an hour he had assembled much more than he would have dared hope for: stimulants, depressants, systemic purifiers, tissue regenerants, ersatz nerves, assimilable skin, synthetic plasma, clotting agents, antiallergens, immunosuppressants, and simple painkillers. Also there were several items of no obvious relevance, such as specifics for Watkins fever and lembrotal withdrawal symptoms.

And most of the instruments appeared intact. That, though, was only on the outside. Inside, they contained fantastically delicate webs of electronic circuitry; solidstate though it was, without the master checkboard to confirm normal functioning, he had to suspect that it might have been deranged by the crash. You didn't pick up a modern diagnostic device and throw it at the wall. If you only let it fall to the floor, you checked it out before re-using it.

And the checkboard had been filled with drifting sand. So even if—as he was half-thinking—he did contrive to jury-rig a power source, he wouldn't be able to rely on it.

Forget the instruments, then, except the most ancient of all, like limb-tractors and scalpels. For thousands of years doctors had had to depend on the data they could carry in their own heads, and by modern standards his mind was well-stocked because he had always been blessed with an atavistically good memory. Just as the invention of writing put paid to the blind bards who could recite ten thousand lines of Homer without prompting, and the invention of computers put paid to the

mathematicians who could multiply ten-digit numbers in their
heads, so the invention of diagnostic tools had discouraged the
kind of doctor who could distinguish five hundred types of fever
by simple inspection. But Pavel had taken a great interest, when
he was a student, in the history of medicine, and he was confi-
dent that most of what he had learned was there in his mind,
ready to be used—

Or was it? Was that a euphoric delusion due to the stimulant
he'd injected into his arm?

He had no way of telling. He could only order himself to proceed very cautiously.

Right: he had a patient waiting, providing he hadn't died in
the meantime. He selected what he thought would prove most
helpful from the pile of drugs and instruments before him and
for want of anything better as a light source added a retinal ex-
amination torch, whose beam was no thicker than his finger
even at maximum spread but was at least nice and bright.

And went back to Andrew's cabin.

As he put out his hand to slide the door back, he was struck
by a terrifying premonition. During his search of the wreck, he
had seen few actual corpses—apart from that disgustingly
squashed body hurled against the end of the corridor—but he
knew the rest of them must be there, under the near-mountain
of sand which had collapsed on the hull.

Suppose while he was gone Andrew *had* died? He was hardly
what you'd call a fit young man; he overindulged in liquor,
probably in drugs too, and certainly he over-ate. He was far too
fat for his age, twenty-two or twenty-three.

If he had died, Pavel would be compelled to wait alone for a
rescue party, with no one to talk to, even if the talking were no
more than an exchange of insults . . . and no proof that he *was*
going to be rescued.

Until this moment, he'd taken rescue for granted. He'd been
aware that they had dropped out of subspace almost an hour
before the explosion, leaving as usual plenty of margin, because
emerging from subspace close to a sun was dangerous and an

old ship like the *Pennyroyal* had to allow some one and a half to two AU when entering a system like this.

This voyage from Halys to Carteret was a routine affair—a milk run, as the ancient argot termed it. Nonetheless, even if Captain Magnusson didn't keep what you would call a tight ship, he would presumably have signaled ahead to tell the port controller on Carteret that they were in real space again. . . .

Presumably.

Pavel felt abruptly ill. No, he was being too kind to the captain—*nil mortuis*. Putting it bluntly, Magnusson had run a sloppy ship, the worst of the dozen or so Pavel had signed aboard. The chances were that the explosion which had wrecked the *Pennyroyal* had been due to neglect of some official safety-precaution. And there was a risk, small but not to be ignored, that Magnusson might have thought signaling ahead to their destination was superfluous.

In which case there might be a long wait before him. A *very* long wait! And if he had to face it on his own—could he stand the strain?

He slammed back the cabin door violently to wipe out the picture which had arisen in his head: the sight of himself, face in the rictus of Hippocrates, surrounded by the empty drug phials he had retrieved from the surgery.

At once a whining voice came to his ears, and he was so relieved by that, he almost failed to pay attention to the words.

"You went away and left me!"

What?

He turned on the torch and approached the bunk. Andrew spoke again.

"You came in before—I heard you! You left me lying in this terrible pain! Damn you, damn you!"

Pavel was about to blurt an angry rejoinder, but he caught himself. Instead he said soothingly, "I went to get some drugs and instruments. You're in a bad way, Andrew."

"You went away and left me alone in the dark!" The voice would have become hysterically loud, but on the last breath it broke into a whimper, and then there were sobs, shrill and grating, like those of a spoiled child denied a piece of candy.

It should have been anyone but Andrew—anyone!

Maybe, though, this petulance was ascribable to his pain, which must be agonizing. That would be dealt with. Pavel selected an injector from the handful he had brought and placed it against Andrew's exposed right arm. A few seconds, and—

"Oh, it's you." As though time had been turned back, the voice had reverted to normal, complete with the sneer he'd learned to detest during their voyage. "The so-called doctor who can't even treat a simple headache!"

That was an allusion to their last encounter. Andrew had called for him—not come to his surgery, like the others—and insisted he had a migraine. Thorough, punctilious, Pavel had checked him out, and his instruments had confirmed what he had already started to suspect: the young man's complaint wasn't migraine at all, but a hangover which had lasted three days without an interlude which might have allowed the body's own defences to flush it away. And he'd said so, adding that Andrew was on the verge of alcoholic poisoning, and Andrew had roared that he was a liar and unfit to practice his profession. He had gone so far as to report Pavel to the captain . . . not that that made much impression. Captain Magnusson, fundamentally, resented the regulation which compelled him to have a medical officer on board at all, and would have been happier with mere machines, since they were cheaper.

Roughly, Pavel said, "You have something a lot worse than a headache."

Andrew's forehead creased. "Why are you shining that light at me? Why is it dark in here?"

"Why the hell do you think? We crashed, of course!"

"Crashed?" Andrew almost sat up—but Pavel put a heavy hand on his shoulder to prevent him.

"Lie still! You have a broken back and probably a broken pelvis, and all kinds of internal injuries. I gave you a painkiller, but if you want to live you absolutely must *not* move."

"What?" Fretfully; Andrew seemed not to have taken in what he'd been told. He made to lift the coverlet, and winced.

"Hell, that hurt! And you said you'd given me a painkiller! Can't you even use the right drug to—"

"Now you listen to me!" Pavel rasped. He was picking among the gear he had brought, looking for the collapsible limb-tractor. "You're about as badly broken as a man can be and still expect to survive. Have you got that?"

"I . . ."

Andrew's face crumpled like a wet paper mask as he realised: *this is happening to me!* He said, "We crashed?"

"Why the hell else do you imagine your bunk is on the wrong side of the cabin? What do you think threw all your belongings across the floor? If you hadn't been in your bunk, but up and about like everybody else, you'd be under a thousand tons of sand!"

"None of your needling! I live the way I choose to live, and if other people don't like it that's their bad luck!"

"Oh, shut up!" Pavel was assembling the limb-tractor now. "Make the most of the painkiller I gave you. There isn't much left, and the only other thing I can do to dull the pain you'd feel without it would be to give you a total block on the lower spinal cord—and I'm not sure it could be reversed. It might mean you being paralyzed. If you want to walk around again, a whole man, you listen to me and do as I say. Clear?"

The blurred oval of Andrew's half-open mouth trembled. He was getting through.

"All right! Now I'm going to have to fix your left arm. It's dislocated, but this will reseat the shoulder in its socket." He hefted the limb-tractor. "So brace yourself. You probably haven't suffered much pain in your life, but human beings used to put up with far worse than what you'll feel. Now if I can get around this bunk to the other side. . . ." Moving as he talked, he found there was just enough room for him to stand.

"They also used to put up with head-lice and fleas and open

sores!" Andrew snapped. "We've made progress since those days!"

Surprised to find that this spoiled young man had even heard of such things, Pavel lifted the desensitized arm and fitted the tractor around it, trying not to think about the nauseatingly wrong angle it made at the shoulder. He said, "There hasn't been much progress here. We seem to be on the next planet out from Carteret. It hasn't even evolved into the Pleistocene Age. Right, here we go!"

And he snapped the spring of the tractor, and the shoulder joint re-engaged with a thud. Perfect.

Detaching the device again, he heard Andrew saying, "Well, what about you, then?" The old acid burned in his tone, as though he were constitutionally incapable of talking to people without seeking ways of making them feel small. "Were you in your bunk too, like me?"

"No! I was thrown clear through the surgery bulkhead and into that compartment full of furs. By a miracle they were all out of their bales, and—"

"Well, hell!" Andrew crowed. "I saved your life!"

"What?" The next stage would be to cleanse and examine the injured man's lower body; Pavel was already selecting the gear he required for the job. He paused and glanced up.

"Saved your life," Andrew repeated with a harsh attempt at a laugh. "I was bored last night. I woke that man—what's his name? The one from the fur dealers?"

"You mean—what *was* his name?" Pavel said glacially. "He's dead."

"I didn't like him anyway," Andrew said. "But I woke him and told him to show off his goods. Made him take them all out of their packing. Well, I'll be damned! If I hadn't done that, you'd have been—"

"Killed," Pavel broke in. "But *you* would have been dying here in terrible pain."

"The hell I would," Andrew said. "That's not my style. You should know that by now."

Worriedly, Pavel stared at him. One of the side-effects of the drug he'd used, in certain susceptible types, was a kind of megalomaniac euphoria. It appeared that Andrew must be susceptible.

"No. Look just to your right," Andrew went on. "See that black case?"

Pavel complied, and noticed a square dark case which he must narrowly have missed treading on when he went around the bunk to apply the limb-tractor. He picked it up. It was heavy for its size.

"There's a combination lock. Press five, two, five, one, four."

With the help of the torch, Pavel did as he was told, and the lid sprang back. His blood ran suddenly cold.

"Know what that is, do you?" Andrew said triumphantly.

"Yes." Pavel heard his voice as gritty as the wind blowing across the dunes outside. "I should have guessed that this was what you meant. It's an Easy Way Out."

Small. No longer, no thicker, than his forearm. But unbelievably expensive. This sleek blue plasteel cylinder with its white cap on one end, bedded in a shock-absorbent lining covered with red velvet, might easily have cost half as much as the *Pennyroyal*.

It was a legal development of an earlier device which had had to be banned because on planet after planet it had stolen the hope of survival from pioneers worn out with their attempts to overcome the infinite problems an alien world could pose. Cynical and cold-blooded entrepreneurs had bought early versions of the machine—which filled half a spaceship—and made fortunes by luring settlers into imaginary universes so delightful they were happy to starve to death rather than give up their next session of pleasure. Several worlds that were now officially freehold in the power of a single family had been, as one might say, "cleared" in this manner.

When the scandal threatened to reach epidemic proportions, Earth's sluggish government had finally enacted a law. By then, however, the profit to be had from using the machines had shrunk; there were few worlds remaining to be grabbed. And in addition miniaturization had—as always—progressed, so that they could be held in one's hand instead of sprawling out through a fifty-metre hold. Also as always the law was a compromise. It was not forbidden to manufacture the things, only to purchase or use them if one was not a bona fide space traveler or engaged in some occupation so dangerous as to involve the risk of fatal accident. In practice, that meant they were sold to space tourists, government officials, and chief officers of spacelines. They were rich.

Activated—and all it required for activation was a twist of the white cap and a firm push—it broadcast a signal direct to the brain of anybody within range, in other words within about a hundred metres. The signal forged a link, so to speak, between the brain's pleasure centres and the memory, diverting the remaining resources of the body into the construction of a delectable dream so absorbing, so convincing, that minor matters like loss of blood, or starvation, or intolerable pain, were instantly forgotten. Trapped in a collapsed mineshaft, sunk beneath an ocean with an hour's worth of air, lost between the stars, one could live out the balance of his life in an ideally happy illusion. According to temperament, it could be erotic—or an orgy of eating—or a tussle with a favourite hallucinogen—or the accomplishment of a lifelong ambition—or . . .

Or anything. Literally, *anything*.

In principle, then, it was a marvelous and humane idea. What fate could be crueller to an aware, sensitive being than knowledge of inescapably impending death? When there was no hope of rescue, better that a man should end his days in unalloyed delight!

Fine.

But the moment that cap was pressed home, it was certain that he *would* end his days. It was a gesture implying suicide. Once those new neural paths had been burned into the cortex, there could never be any retreat from death.

According to what Pavel had read, this had not been true of

the earliest versions. One could recover from those, as one could from the ancient addictive drugs, at the cost of incredible self-discipline and long, slow, painstaking psychiatric help. With a model as advanced as the one he held now . . . no.

He shut the lid and jumbled the lock again, and carefully placed the case on a shelf where Andrew could not reach it.

"What are you doing?" Andrew cried. "You said you knew what it was! Can't you turn it on?"

"Yes." Pavel averted his face and focused his little torch on his medical gear, making a great business of picking out what he would need to complete the job he had barely started.

"Then. . . !"

"Oh, shut up!" With a fury that appalled him—it was no tone for a doctor to use to a patient. "Or I'll shut you up!" He grasped an anesthetic injector, not local like the one he had already administered, designed to inactivate pain-nerves selectively, but one which would blot out the whole nervous system. "In fact"—with growing resolution—"I guess I'll do that anyway!"

And clapped the injector against Andrew's arm.

"You bastard!" Andrew husked. "You devil! You . . . !"

On the last word his voice failed. His eyes, glinting in the pale beam of the torch, shut against his will, and seconds later he slumped inert.

It's kinder, anyway. . . .

But Pavel knew, even as he pulled the coverlet from the bunk and mechanically began to occupy himself with the foul job of cleaning excrement and dried blood from Andrew's lower body, that that was not the truth. There had been as much violence in that act as if he had given Andrew a punch on the jaw. And the reason why he needed to let his violence erupt—

Well, even though his mind was preoccupied with his work, even though the effect of the stimulant injection he had given himself was half used up by the low-oxygen air and the hunger which now—paradoxically—was making his stomach growl audibly, he was able to reason it out. He was scared out of his wits.

He was very young by modern standards, if not as young as Andrew, being only thirty-five and looking forward to a probable lifetime of at least a hundred and twenty. Proportionately, he *vis-à-vis* Andrew was in the same situation as a man just come of age at twenty-one would have been when dealing with a twelve- or thirteen-year-old boy before mankind began to colonize other solar systems: very much aware of the drawbacks of being adolescent because they were still so fresh in his own memory, yet terribly impatient with the consequences of being adolescent because he was so exhausted by having gradually conquered them in himself.

As though imposing a penance on himself for his surrender to anger and fear, he made a particularly thorough and careful job of the cleansing process, undertaking manually some of the most revolting parts which he could have used an instrument for, assuming the instrument was working after the crash. Eventually, however, he decided that the stimulant was wearing off completely, and he ought not to take a second dose before eating.

By then he had done absolutely all he had the resources to do: Andrew was in a spider's web of medical devices, two or three of which he had had to return to the surgery to bring, which would minimize pain, extract fatigue poisons direct through the skin, cleanse him whenever his bowels and bladder leaked, and insure him against the vanishingly small risk of some degenerative infection such as gangrene. Provided rescue arrived within fifteen days, he should not merely survive, but survive in good enough health to endure the major operation on his spine necessary to restore his power of ambulation. It was an achievement to be proud of, especially since Pavel had been prevented from using so many of his regular tools owing to the risk of them suffering damage in the crash.

Now it was high time he thought about himself . . . as clearly as the air would allow him to.

He was thirsty, he realized, not just dry from the arid air of this planet but actually dehydrated from his hard work. He had a number of phials of distilled water in the surgery, including several of litre capacity which had been so well-packaged they remained intact, and he had a fair supply of glucose solution and other instant-energy concentrates, various stimulants which rapidly invoked the "second wind" process in muscle tissue, many different tablets and capsules which, although intended exclusively for metabolic tests, could be used as nutriment in emergency, and even a range of chemicals that generated free oxygen which he could use if the sparse natural air and the pressure of excess CO_2 were handicapping him for some really urgent task.

But so long as he could manage without drawing on those supplies, the better his chances would be of lasting until rescue arrived. He would rather starve until a ship came down to collect him, and leave with a store of unused supplies behind him, than . . .

Or—would he?

He sat down, only half-intending to, on a stool which had surprisingly remained upright in the tangle of the surgery, and remembered to shut off the torch he was carrying. A little light, now very red because the sun was setting, showed his surroundings to him. He faced, at long last, the fundamental reason for his . . . his *attack* on Andrew.

He didn't believe with his whole being that he was going to be rescued. He didn't believe that anything would be done to organize search parties until the *Pennyroyal* was so much more overdue than the normal range of variation in her schedule that somebody on Carteret grew angry. He hadn't made many trips with Magnusson's ship, but he was well aware that a difference of a week or two one way or the other in their time of docking on any given planet which the ship serviced didn't seem to worry the captain. Unless he could improvise a beacon, preferably a powerful radio beacon. . . .

And he was trained in medicine, not engineering or electronics. If he was reluctant to use his own professional aids because he feared they might have been rendered unreliable, how could he trust a radio or subspace signaller even if he managed to rout one out from the mass of sand engulfing the after part of the ship and connect it to a power supply? How would he know whether it was crying for help, or simply lighting up the state-of-circuit lamps?

He thought of the daunting process of shovelling sand away, encountering corpses, being frustrated because food capsules had smashed open and the contents were uneatable, which he had to undergo if he was really determined to survive.

And then thought of the Easy Way Out.

Yes, that was what was frightening him, more than the risk of dying here, forgotten, on an uninhabited world.

If he had not known that the EWO existed, if he had been able to occupy himself solely with problems of survival, he might have made it. As things stood, knowing that the choice lay between an agonizing death and a delightful one, he—

"NO!"

It astonished him that he shouted it aloud, and leapt to his feet in the same moment. Something in the very depths of his mind had said: *I don't want to die at all.*

That made sense. He didn't want to be here on Quasimodo IV. He didn't want to have a vast ache all down his legs and a twisted ankle and a dry throat and particularly he didn't want a patient who insulted him when he was trying to help. But he did want to live. With almost three-quarters of a lifetime ahead of him, he hated the idea that he might be doomed by someone's damn-fool carelessness!

Unsteadily, head pounding, with only the pencil beam of the torch to guide him, he set off on a second exploration of the ship.

Hours passed. His watch was working, but he had forgotten to check it when he awoke after the crash, and when it did occur to him to look at it he found it wasn't much use. It had been set to the arbitrary ship's day, and assured him the "real" time was a few minutes before noon. Only the star-spangled sky of which he caught occasional glimpses remained dark, and he vaguely remembered seeing somewhere that the day of this planet was much longer than Earth's, well over thirty hours. So it wouldn't even be possible to predict dawn until he had seen one, and another sunset.

But that was a minor matter. He had biological clocks in his body which were more important, and the loudest-chiming one was in his belly. He was sure that by now his increasing weakness was due less to lack of oxygen and his many bruises than to simple hunger. And, inescapably, thirst.

Accordingly he directed his first efforts at digging towards where he knew the ship's restaurant had been located, on the side of the hull opposite his surgery. But this had been crushed far worse than the other side, and the sand was piled high and spilled down to replace whatever he scrabbled away. He was on the brink of despair when he recognized something shining in the beam of the torch.

Sand-scraped, the label told him plainly: WHOLE MILK.

He seized the bulbous can and raised it to his lips, ignoring the sand which clogged the outlet. The sand was presumably sterile, and if it wasn't, he'd already been exposed over and over to whatever minor life-forms it bore. He gulped the milk down in huge draughts, thinking with a detached portion of his mind that there was—or should have been—something symbolic in this action.

But this planet was not one which he could envisage substituting for Mother Earth.

After that he found a whole group of similar containers, apparently the contents of a shelf which had been slammed through a bulkhead in the crash. Many of them were crushed and had leaked their contents, but he recovered more milk, various types of consommé and broth, and five or six types of purée. Beyond, there was a mess of fresh fruit, including apples, papayas and a mutated citrus he was fond of, called yabanos, resembling a lime bloated to the size of an orange and with deep pink flesh. He eagerly tore at its peel, and had already set a chunk of it to his lips when he realized what his sense of touch had been trying to warn him about: the crash had hurled this fruit into something made of glass, and the glass had smashed. The whole of it was permeated with tiny sharp spikes.

He spat it out and threw it away in fury. If this was what was going to happen everywhere, he might as well—

NO! NO! At least this time he didn't shout it aloud, but he said it inside his head, very forcibly: *I am not going to take the Easy Way Out! I am not! I am NOT!*

And then honesty which he detested compelled him to add: *At least . . . I don't think I am.*

He took one final look at Andrew, who was still unconscious, and gave him an injectorful of glucose-and-vitamin booster. He had found a few phials of that intact, and there were also some high-protein concentrates and other life-supports. But Andrew was carrying enough fat on his belly to last him several days, and he certainly wasn't going to become dehydrated overnight . . . or whatever the equivalent of "overnight" might be, measured in terms of how long it took Pavel to wake up after he collapsed on his pile of furs. His own cabin, far astern in the crew's quarters, was unreachable, but a dozen furs in the corridor afforded a soft bed within earshot of Andrew if he recovered consciousness.

The rest . . .
could wait . . .
until later. . . .

"Turn it on! Damn you—damn you! *Turn it on!*"
Pavel came awake in a second. The cry, eerie in the echoing corridor, had seemed a continuation of the dream he had been suffering, a vision of endless wandering over a vast bare desert. He forced himself to his feet, aware of the nasty clinging of his clothes to his body—normally, he changed them twice a day and threw the worn ones in the recycler, but that was smashed. At least during the night a breeze must have blown away the stench left by the fires inside the ship; the air now, although still very dry and oxygen-poor, smelled of nothing at all.
When he lay down to sleep, he had set the torch and a num-

ber of flasks and medical phials nearby. Now, though, he did not need artificial light—the sun must be well up in the sky and pouring in through all the cracks in the hull—and he was too dazed to worry about the other things. He stumbled into Andrew's cabin rubbing his eyes.

Calm overtook him as he saw the medical equipment he had rigged yesterday. Being self-powered, against failure of the ship's power, its state-of-operation lights continued to gleam like little reptile's eyes. And indicated no change worth noticing in Andrew's condition: metabolism survival-prone, skeletal structure paralysis-prone, nervous system pain-prone. . . .

"That! That thing!"

Andrew shouted, as loudly as he could, and raised his right arm to point at the shelf where Pavel had set the EWO.

"Turn it on!"

Pavel drew a deep breath. His head felt as though it had been stuffed with sand from outside, his mouth as dry and harsh as though the sand had been inserted by that route, and his stomach was full of gas-bloat. Also his ankle seemed to have become worse during his sleep, not better, and when he rested his weight on it he winced.

Reaching out, he took the EWO off the shelf and wordlessly carried it from the cabin. Behind him, Andrew screamed and howled.

It occurred to Pavel that he should pitch the EWO out of the ship altogether, into the sand, where night wind would cover it and make it impossible to find again. But even as he was tensing his muscles to toss the thing away, he relented. Rescue, after all, might *not* come. . . .

Of the many cupboards in his surgery, all had been flung open in the crash, but one had not had its doors torn off the hinges. He put the EWO inside and slammed the doors and twisted the lock shut, thinking as he did so: *out of sight, out of . . .*

My mind?

But he didn't want to think about that. He had dreamed about it.

When he returned to Andrew's cabin he heard, from several metres away, a helpless moaning noise. He hurried his last few steps, and there indeed was Andrew with his hands over his face, weeping.

"Okay, okay!" Pavel said, and touched the younger man's arm reassuringly. "I'm here, and I have my—"

"Turn it on!" Andrew repeated, his hands muffling the words.

"I've taken the EWO away," Pavel said, and waited.

"What?" The hands dropped from Andrew's tear-wet face. "But it's mine! If I tell you to turn it on you've got to turn it on! I can't bear to lie here and suffer this *pain!*"

"Would you rather throw away the rest of your life," Pavel said after a moment to ponder the right form of words, "than survive to enjoy all these things you kept boasting about on the trip—all the money, the luxury, the power your family's possessions will bring you?"

"I . . ."

Andrew hesitated, letting his arms fall to his sides. He looked with fear-filled eyes at the medical equipment enclosing his body from the waist down.

Pavel went on waiting.

Abruptly—and unexpectedly—Andrew said, "I guess if you don't have too much anesthetic left you'd better save it for when I start to scream. But do you have a tranquilizing shot?"

A wave of relief swept over Pavel. He had never heard Andrew speak in such a reasonable tone before. He said, "Sure. Not much of that is left, either, though. My whole stock of drug phials was thrown through the surgery bulkhead along with me, and even if some of them were saved from breaking by landing in the furs it'll take a while for me to dig them out. Here's something to be going on with, at least."

He selected the right injector from the mixed batch he had brought, and applied it.

"Thank you," Andrew said, even before it had taken effect. "I—I guess I should apologise for shouting at you, hm?"

Pavel shrugged.

"How are you?"

"Me?" Pavel's surprise showed in his voice. "Oh . . . oh, I'm not too bad."

"I asked you a question! Don't I deserve an answer?"

"Well . . ." Pavel licked his lips. "My head aches like fury, but I guess yours does too. It's the air. My throat is sore, but that's the air too—it's very dry. When the crash came I acquired a gang of bruises and a twisted ankle. Now you know. And as a doctor I can promise you I'm in far better shape than you are."

"Obviously." A ghost of a smile showed on Andrew's pale plump face. "I'm in the kind of mess it would take a major hospital to cope with, aren't I?"

Pavel nodded. There was no point in trying to conceal the truth.

"Then why the *hell* won't you turn on the EWO?" Andrew blasted.

Pavel froze. He said at last, "You spoiled brat. You—you . . . oh, I don't know a name bad enough for you!"

"Now look here!" Andrew began, but Pavel plunged on.

"Before you try any more of your tricks, get this into your solid plasteel head, will you? I want to stay alive even if you don't! You've been pampered all your life so much that even a hint of pain makes you want to give up forever. You can't con me into doing what you want, you can't threaten me into doing what you want, you can't wheedle me into doing what you want. For once in your life you are simply going to have to do what someone else wants!"

There was a dead silence. Since Pavel had woken, the whole ship had been silent, apart from the soughing of a light wind across the gaps in the hull. The trickling noise he had heard yesterday in the surgery, the sifting noise of sand filling a few remaining spaces in the after part of the ship, the creaking of the girders as they cooled—all that had come to an end. The only items in operation, the medical equipment, were too efficiently designed to make a noise even after the punishment they had taken.

Then the artificial calm of the last shot he had been given overspread Andrew's face. He said, "Well, if you're so determined to keep me alive, you might as well make me comfortable too. I'm in pain, you know."

"All right," Pavel conceded. "But I'll have to make it a short dose. I'll have to accustom you gradually to supporting some of your pain, I'm afraid. There's no way of estimating how long it will be before we're rescued." He produced and applied the correct injector.

"And I'm afraid I can't be absolutely certain how badly your internal organs are affected," he went on. "To be on the safe side, I'll have to keep you hydrated with an intravenous transfusion rather than letting you drink."

"But I'm very thirsty," Andrew said in a dull tone, his eyes drifting shut.

"I guess you must be. I have some tablets you can suck to keep your mouth and throat moist, but they'll have to be rationed out, too."

"Because we may be stuck here a long time," Andrew murmured. "What make you so sure we are going to be rescued, hm?"

"Look, we're in the same system as Carteret," Pavel said. "We're going to be reported overdue. If there was a live detector anywhere in the vicinity, it will have picked up our blip. It might even have tracked us to impact."

"Hell, if it tracked us to impact, no one will bother to come searching," Andrew said. "Everyone was killed but us, right? If they calculate the speed we had when we broached air, they'll take it for granted we just burned up!"

Pavel was half-convinced of that himself, but he put on his most reassuring manner.

"Not if I can dig out something to make a beacon with," he said. "I'm not an engineer, but I hope to find a solid-state transmitter sooner or later, and a capacitor or something to drive it with. I'll—uh—I'll leave you now and get on with it."

"Thirsty!" Andrew said.

"Oh, of course. I'll get you one of those tablets to suck."

Behind the closed cupboard doors the presence of the EWO seemed to mock him when he entered the surgery.

Then, having made a frugal breakfast from half a can of fruit purée, Pavel sat down to work out a plan. In this sparse air he dared not over-exert himself; on the other hand, he must work quickly in order to improve their chances of survival, either to fix the beacon he'd talked about or simply to locate more provisions.

In a while, despite his aching head, he had what seemed to be a logical course of action. He hunted around for something he could adapt as a shovel, found a plastic chair with one metal leg still attached and, by wedging the leg in a crack in the wall and leaning on it with his full weight, straightened it so that the chair-seat made a kind of flat scoop, and the leg a handle. Fine. Very pleased with himself, he set about digging where he had found the bulbs of soup yesterday.

And almost at once discovered a mangled corpse.

The thought crossed his mind that if he absolutely had to, he could reserve the canned supplies until last, and eat meat. It should remain good for a long time in this dry air, away from Earth-type bacteria.

Revolting! cried his subconscious. *Better the EWO than cannibalism!*

Maybe.

He moved the body and with much effort dragged it to a gash in the hull, and pushed it outside. He scrambled after it, dragged it out of sight down the dune and flung a few shovelfuls of sand after it. Then, aching in every limb, he decided to walk around the ship instead of going straight back inside. The going was very difficult; the dune was so dry, he sank in over his ankles at every step. But he managed to carry out a complete inspection of the exposed part of the ship, and the more he saw, the more he marvelled at his own escape. A bare fifth of the vessel's length was visible, and as badly cracked as a hard-boiled egg ready for shelling. His heart sank. Was there any hope at all of finding serviceable equipment to rig his beacon?

Well, there was only one way to find out. He went back to his digging.

After that, time passed in a monotonous slow blur. He fell immediately into the routine which he was to follow for the whole of their stay. He dug for a while, making either the discovery of a corpse or the location of a bit of intact equipment the excuse to break off, and then went to see Andrew and attend to his requests or—more and more often—inform him that they couldn't be met right now, because there were only a handful of injectors left, or the medical equipment reported that it would be dangerous to give him more liquid by mouth, or there was some other reason for denying him what he wanted.

The first time he told Andrew he would have to lie in pain a bit longer before another shot, Andrew curled his lip back and said, "I've got you figured out. You like this."

"What?"

"You like this. You like having someone totally helpless, the way I am. Gives you a sense of power!"

Sweat beaded his face, but evaporated almost at once into the dry air.

"Nonsense!" Pavel said roughly, looking over the equipment at the foot of the bunk. One of the lights which had been green had turned red. But there was no help for that.

"Oh, I know your type!" Andrew snapped. "Nothing suits you better than—"

"Shut up," Pavel said. "I'm trying to keep us both alive. And, if possible, sane. Don't start on crazy fantasies like that, or you'll run the risk of making me angry. And I'm already living on my nerves."

"So what does a doctor do when his patient makes him angry? Turn off the life-supports?"

"No." Pavel drew a deep but unsatisfying breath. "Gets out of earshot of the goading, and stays there."

He marched out of the cabin and slammed the door. In the corridor he leaned for a while against the wall, head on hands. If this was going to go on indefinitely . . .

But there was work to do. He roused himself and returned to it. Not for the first time as he mustered all his energy and thrust the improvised shovel into yet another heap of sand, he wondered sickly why he was wasting his time. He was now well into the section where he ought to have located usable electronic or subelectronic equipment if any had survived, and all he was finding was charred or half-melted masses of metal and plastic. There had been a fire here, and a hot one. Also, now and then, he found items from spacemen's uniform, such as buckles and rank badges. And there were bones.

It took him almost three days—daytimes, rather—to clear the section of the ship of which he had the highest hopes. The only thing he found which was any use at all was a solid-state emergency lamp, its lumen-globe intact and its powerpack barely below maximum. When he came upon it, night was falling. He switched it on, thinking how wonderful it was to have a proper light.

And then, with a pang of conscience, how terrible it must be for Andrew lying alone in the dark, forced to wait hours between anesthetic shots. He picked the lamp up and carried it to Andrew's cabin.

He was dozing, and did not at first react to the sound of the door sliding back—it moved noisily now, because the finest grains of sand sifted everywhere when the wind rose, and the groove at the bottom was covered with them. When he opened his eyes, however, he did not comment on the lamp.

He said, "Pavel, you—you look terrible!"

"What?" Pavel touched his face. He had three days' stubble on it, of course, and no doubt dirt and sweat had mingled to cover his skin with a layer of grime . . . but he hadn't given the point a thought for a long while.

"Could be," he said gruffly. "But never mind. Here, I found this lamp. I thought it would be useful for you. I could get you something to pass the time now you have light. Uh—maybe a book, if you like reading. Or a game from the recreation room. I dug into that and found a few things."

But Andrew seemed not to be listening. He said, "Why in the galaxy are you driving yourself this way? Did you find a way to send a signal to a search party?"

"Uh . . ." Pavel licked his lips; they tasted of dust. "I found quite a lot of stuff already, but—"

"But it doesn't work?"

"No, I'm afraid it's all smashed up."

"I thought it would be," Andrew said. Now, by the bright clear light, Pavel could see that his cheeks had suddenly become sunken, and there was another lamp shining red on the medical gear enclosing his legs, which yesterday had been green. Red for danger. "Pavel, you ought at least to leave the EWO where I can get at it! Suppose—well, suppose you dig into somewhere and a girder falls on you? Suppose you're hurt and can't get back to wherever you put the thing?"

"I don't want to use it," Pavel said obstinately.

"And you won't keep me free of pain all the time!"

"I can't because—"

"Oh, save it!" Andrew sighed, and rolled his head to the side opposite the lamp, shutting his eyes again.

The ungrateful bastard, Pavel thought, and strode out.

That night, like the previous nights, he dropped off to sleep the moment he lay down on his couch of furs in the passageway outside Andrew's door. He dreamed of far-off worlds where he had been happy and relaxed, where he had basked in warm sunlight and eaten luscious meals in the company of pretty women, where—

Has Andrew somehow got at the EWO and turned it on?

That thought blasted through the euphoria of his dreams and

brought him bolt upright with a jerk. Standing up and waking
were simultaneous. It was dark; he had turned off the lamp to
conserve its powerpack, Andrew being asleep also. But he had
left it on a shelf just inside the cabin door, and the door was
ajar. He located it by touch and switched it on.

Andrew was lying, very pale, sweating again, with his fists
clenched and his jaw set, and another red light had appeared at
the foot of his bunk.

"Damn it, you're in agony!" Pavel burst out.

"I didn't want to—to—wake you," Andrew forced between
his tightly clamped teeth. "Thought you—you deserved your
rest."

What in the galaxy was happening to this spoiled young
man? But Pavel wasted no time on wondering about that. He
had, as usual, placed a selection of drug phials and other equipment by his couch. Seizing a painkiller injector, he gave Andrew
a full shot.

"Thanks," the younger man whispered, and the drawn expression faded from his face. "Sorry I disturbed you. I guess I
cried out without meaning to."

"That's okay," Pavel said awkwardly.

"You know something?" Andrew went on, staring at the ceiling. "I've been thinking. I guess I never had to think so long
about the same thing, over and over, in my life before. When
the crash happened, I was so scared. I didn't realize. I kept telling myself it couldn't possibly be happening to me—not to Andrew Alighieri Solichuk–Fehr! And ... well, the way I see it
now, I went on trying to hide the truth. Didn't I? Don't bother
to answer. I know I'm right now. And here you've been working
like a—like a robot, and knowing what can be done and what
can't, and ... well, imagine it had been the other way around!
Imagine that I'd been up and walking about, and you were
stuck in a bunk like me, busted all to hell. I wouldn't know what
to do! I'd go crazy! I'd have just turned the cap of the EWO and
given up."

Pavel listened, hardly believing his ears.

"So I . . . well, I'd just like to say I'm obliged to you. I think it's the most amazing luck that you were the other person who survived. It's finally dawned on me that without you I'd be dead."

His fists clenched again, but not—this time—from pain.

"And you're right! It's stupid to die when you don't have to! It's stupid to quit just because you can't take a little pain, just because you're gambling on the chance of being rescued and you can't figure the odds! Hell, I've gambled on a dozen planets, for things much less important than life—for mere money! And I swear I wouldn't have bet on my chance of still being alive after that crash!"

"Nor would I," Pavel said in a gravelly tone. From the corner of his eye he noted that the last red light had reverted to green, a sign that it had been the pain which was putting the dangerous stress on Andrew's metabolism. Dilemma: whether to keep the pain damped down, in order to protect his life-functions, or to husband the supply of painkiller and make his life bearable, if not comfortable, for the greatest possible length of time. . . .

It was too much to think about right now, his mind still muzzy with sleep. Anyhow, Andrew hadn't finished.

"You're sure we're on Quasimodo IV?"

"Ah . . ." Until this moment, Pavel hadn't been certain that Andrew had taken in the information he'd been given about their situation. "Yes. At least, as sure as I can be without checking out some sort of data on the system we were bound for. I haven't dug into a library section yet, but I think I'm coming fairly close."

"Well, instead of wasting my time on games and that sort of nonsense, why don't you bring me what you can salvage in the way of books and reels? I guess if there's a magnifying glass or microscope to be had, I can make out a reel. But without power there can't be much hope of reading tapes, hm?"

"True enough. But—sure, I'll do my best. Find some way of magnifying a reel so you can read it up against that light."

"Great," Andrew said. "Now you go back to sleep, or fix your

breakfast, or whatever you want. I'll be okay until this shot
wears off. And I'll try and be okay until a good while afterwards. Just as long as I can honestly stand the pain."

Fantastic! Pavel kept thinking as he burrowed deeper and
deeper into the accessible regions of the ship. *To have found that
degree of guts when he must be in agony!*

It helped—helped enormously—to know that he had a companion in adversity after all, someone he could talk to instead of
a burden on his time, a constant worry. He did in fact locate a
scratched and broken piece of transpex with a high magnifying
factor, and some data reels and a few scorched books whose
pages had to be turned very carefully in order to prevent them
crumbling, and Andrew, propped up just a little on his pillow,
somehow contrived to read a few of them by the portable lamp.
There were only passing references to Quasimodo IV—it never
having been a planet of much interest to spacemen—but what
little he gleaned confirmed that that was where they were, and
moreover that they were currently on the same side of the local
sun as Carteret.

But in that case . . .
Why haven't we been rescued already?

The fourth, fifth, eighth day melted into the past, almost fea-
tureless. Now, the long strain of working in low oxygen was
weakening Pavel; he hated waking up, and often his digging reduced to the mindless act of a machine, so that he had already
shovelled aside a piece of potentially useful equipment before his
sluggish brain recognized it. Then he had to go scrabble for it
with bare hands in the pile of sand behind him. And, of course,
all the time he kept finding dead bodies.

For a brief while, following Andrew's remarkable discovery of
courage, the cupboard where he had stored the EWO held no
threat to Pavel. A day, two days, later, and the blisters on his
hands and the grit in his mouth and the redness of his eyes and
the endless, incurable thirst he suffered from, conspired to re-
awaken its spectre in his memory. Instead of being here, vic-

tim of harsh reality, he could be in a lovely imaginary world, enjoying himself in any way he chose, picturing the most beautiful girls, the smoothest lawns, the finest beaches, the—

Stop it!

But the supply of drugs dwindled, though he hoarded them carefully, and so did the protein concentrates and glucose-and-vitamin solutions which were all the food he could offer Andrew. Luckily, he had had just enough of a substance which triggered the body's use of stored fat—a short-cut for overindulgent passengers, basically, who now and then realized at the end of a long space flight that they had put on two kilos while they were shut up in the metal shell of the ship and wanted to revert to normal before landing. He had never expected to make practical use of what he ordinarily regarded as a cosmetic drug. The two injections of it which he had given to Andrew, however, had worked well, and though his skin was now deflated over his premature paunch, like a partly shrunk balloon, he was able to utilise what long over-indulgence had stored between his muscles and his skin.

Pavel took more and more frequently to going outside and staring up at the sky, knowing it was ridiculous to do so. One couldn't see an orbiting rescue ship by day, and if it arrived during the night it would no doubt fire signal flares and perhaps sonic missiles to wake survivors up and provoke them into lighting fires, or somehow revealing their presence.

Fires!

That idea should have come to him much earlier; in fact, it didn't strike him until finally he had to concede that further digging was useless. The part of the ship he hadn't yet cleared of sand was collapsed, and he lacked the strength, and the tools, to force aside the strong metal girders now blocking his progress.

He had been aimlessly postponing the admission that there was nothing else constructive he could do, when the notion of making a fire occurred to him. At night, in particular, a fire could be spotted a long way off under such a clear sky. He had seen clouds only once since the crash, and they had been on the horizon around the setting sun. Presumably there was ocean in that direction, but a rise in the ground—a range of hills or mountains—filtered all the moisture from the wind before it blew this far inland.

Andrew had found scant reference to the meterological pattern of Quasimodo IV in the charred books Pavel brought him. So many page-edges were burned away, so many details that might have been useful had gone up in smoke!

But was there anything left which would flame brightly in this thin air? Pavel made tests, cautiously, with flammable liquids from his surgery: alcohol, ether, some otherwise useless tinctures and suspensions which bore fire warnings on their labels. Satisfied that it might indeed be possible to light a fire if the fuel were first soaked with everything he had which burned, he set about re-sifting the great mounds of rubbish he had thrown aside, dividing them into two new categories: things that would catch alight, and things that wouldn't.

That occupied a day or two more.

Little by little, however, he began to find himself obsessed with the passage of time. He kept saying under his breath, "Now if we can last out four more days—three more days . . ."

Until, with a shock, he caught himself. There still was no promise of rescue. In his mind, the fifteen-day period he had estimated as the limit of the time he could keep Andrew alive had evolved into an article of faith. *If we last out fifteen days we'll be okay.*

What grounds did he have for believing that? On the contrary, he realized, now that eleven, twelve, thirteen days had leaked away, their chances of being saved were less, not more. Even if Magnusson had been notoriously sloppy about routine matters such as signalling to the port he was bound for when his ship broached normal from subspace, they should have started searching long ago . . . if any detector had picked the *Pennyroyal* up.

It followed that Magnusson hadn't signalled. They could have been eclipsed behind this damned desert planet when they emerged from faster-than-light mode, in which case detectors orbiting Carteret would not have recorded a blip. And their plight was hopeless after all!

The vision of the EWO shut in the cupboard rose before him and sang an inaudible song of mockery.

Weakened by his efforts, and short oxygen and barely sufficient food, he had taken to spending an hour or two each day between exhaustion and slumber in conversation with Andrew. The first few times had been a sort of stimulant for him; he had never had any clear conception of what life was like for someone who was due to inherit one of the great fortunes of the galaxy, coming as he did from average, ordinary stock on both sides of his own family: pioneers five generations back, who seemed to have used up their lines' ambition and initiative in the single crucial act of leaving Earth, and never regained it.

He himself, by deciding to sign as a space medical officer before settling to a regular career, and moreover saying that it might not be on his home world of Caliban that he chose to practice, had shocked all his relatives. They weren't geared to star-travel any more. By contrast, Andrew's background since he was born had included the concept of galaxy-roaming: "Uncle Herbert is on Halys and sends his love," or maybe, "I think we'll take the kids to Peristar this year."

Not that Andrew himself had appreciated his good fortune until now. He had looked on it rather as a distasteful duty than a reason for excitement and enjoyment when he was instructed to go tour the family holdings.

Now, listening to Pavel explaining his attitude, he seemed to have come around to the view that he'd been stupid, wasting an opportunity thousands, millions of young men would have sold their right arms for. Head constantly aching, unceasingly shaky on his feet and having to concentrate with all his force like a man struggling to pretend he isn't drunk, Pavel had done his best to encourage Andrew . . . until the evening of the day when he admitted to himself that even if they did last out for the two weeks he'd invented as a deadline they were probably doomed anyhow.

Then, he was snappish and ill-tempered, heard his own voice reviving accusations from the *Pennyroyal*'s last voyage—references to Hans, references to drunkenness, references to laziness and greed and lack of consideration for other passengers. Hurt, at first surprised, later angry, Andrew retorted in kind, and the should-have-been friendly chat wound up with a grinding slam of the cabin door.

But the last thing Pavel had glimpsed as it shut was not just one more red light—he'd grown accustomed to one a day, on average, added to the original total—but a whole new cluster of them, which yesterday had been green.

Shaking from head to foot, he waited in the corridor for as long as it took to calm himself. Then he reopened the door.

"I'm sorry," he said. "I'm ashamed of myself. You're in terrible pain. The lights . . ." He gestured at them. They were naturally turned away from the patient, so he shouldn't see them.

"I know," Andrew muttered.

"What?"

"Of course I know!" With renewed anger. "That machine of yours wasn't designed to be used in a completely dark room, but a hospital ward with twilight oozing out of the walls—right? Every night when you switch off the lamp for me to go to sleep, I can see the light reflected over there"—gesturing—"and I can tell that it's more red than it was before. I know I'm in a bad way, for heaven's sake! I *know!*"

The last word peaked into a cry.

Pavel bit his lip. He said, "I guess I haven't been completely honest with you. I . . . well, I no longer believe in being rescued. If we were going to be rescued it ought to have happened by now. Do you want me to—?"

"Switch on the EWO?" Andrew broke in. "No! No! And no again! You were right to take it away from me. Lying here, pain or no pain, I've come to realize how precious life can be. No, I don't want you to use it. Take it out and bury it—smash it with a hammer—anything!"

But his voice cracked with pain, and sweat glistened on his skin.

"Well—uh—all right then," Pavel said. "Uh—good night."

"Good night."

Pavel dreamed about the EWO again.

And then, in the morning, the nightmares didn't stop.

When he opened the cabin door, having slept badly and twice having had to force himself to stay awake for ten or fifteen minutes so that when he dropped off again he would not drift straight back into the horrors he had fought to free himself from, he found Andrew not just asleep but unconscious. All but four of the lights on the medical equipment had gone to red. A glance at their pattern confirmed that it was the struggle to resist pain which had worn him out—that, and the exhaustion of the last phial of nutrient solution in Pavel's limited stock. There was enough water left to keep him hydrated, and enough tissue in his muscles for the "second wind" process to keep his basal metabolism turning over for a few more hours—perhaps a couple of days, if he remained inert.

Beyond that point . . .

Certain death.

Pavel stared in giddy disbelief. He tried to tell himself that it was an achievement to have kept Andrew alive and conscious, in his condition, for such a long time—not fifteen ordinary days, as he had somehow been fool enough to imagine, but fifteen of these extra-long local days. It was a medical miracle, in its small way. Hardly any modern doctor could have managed it without the aid of a full range of diagnostic and supportive equipment.

But what was the use of having done it, when nobody else would ever find out?

All hope seeped out of his mind. All his overstrained will to survive collapsed, like a bridge required to carry too great a load: folding, almost gracefully, into an unrecognizable tangle of struts and pillars. He was barely Pavel Williamson any longer as he turned with machine-precise movements and headed for his surgery.

In that cupboard he had passed so many times, the Easy Way Out.

He took it, sleek and chill, from its case, having no difficulty in remembering the combination of its lock, and turned it over and over. It was well past dawn, and there was plenty of light to see it by.

I denied him this, Pavel thought. *I could have ended his life in ecstasy instead of a vain, stupid, pointless struggle against pain. Now he will die, unconscious, and—and he turned out to be a nice guy, in his way. I feel almost fond of him . . . and horribly ashamed of myself.*

Because I'm going to use what I forbade him to.

Convulsively, he twisted the white cap of the EWO and pressed it down. It sank visibly along the main shaft, and there was a humming. Pavel closed his eyes.

Disbelievingly, he opened them again. All was exactly as it had been. Except the EWO. Heavy in his hands, it was now also growing hot. And—

He let it fall with an oath. A hissing noise followed, and a puff of smoke spurted from the capped end. The cap—some kind of plastic, he guessed—deformed and darkened.

After that it simply lay there.

He stared at it incredulously for a long while: how long, he could not tell. He felt like a suicide who took much trouble over choosing and knotting a rope, only to have it break under his weight.

"I'll be damned!" he said furiously at last. "For all that pretty case with the combination lock—for all the padding it was nested in—it broke when we crashed! It doesn't work!"

The thing was no longer smoking. He touched it, and found it merely warm. Snatching it up, he swung around to leave the surgery, blind with rage.

"I'll pay him back for leading me on this way!" he heard himself shouting. "I'll get even! I'll . . ."

What was that?

From somewhere outside, a roaring sound. The crumpled steel of the corridor vibrated. He stood stock-still, one hand already outstretched to slide back the door of Andrew's cabin.

The roar faded, and then grew louder again. He stared in horror at the EWO in his hand, thinking: *Did it work after all? Is this an induced illusion, the fantasy of rescue?*

But, surely, knowing how ashamed he had been when he was finally driven to try and use the gadget, he could rule that out. Any illusion he was capable of enjoying would exclude all memory of the EWO, because even to recall its existence would remind him he was condemned to death . . .

Uncertain, he turned around—and was suddenly running at full lung-tearing pelt towards the nearest opening in the hull, to light his beacon with trembling fingers and keel over beside it for the rescue party to locate.

"I—uh—I guess someone should apologize for not coming to find you sooner," said the doctor at the central hospital on Carteret. "But it was logical enough that all hope was abandoned the moment they computed the *Pennyroyal's* course. I mean, you wouldn't expect anyone to live through a crash like that, hm?"

"I guess not," Pavel said. He felt very much better although this oxygen-rich air was still making him a trifle giddy. "And when they did turn up, it was only for salvage, right? Not for rescue?"

"I'm afraid so," the doctor admitted. "It was the insurance company covering that consignment of furs who chartered the ship which picked you up."

He hesitated. "By the way," he continued at last, "I'd like to compliment you on the marvelous job you did on Andrew Solichuck. You know his family is very big here on Carteret, and if he'd been found dead . . ." He ended the sentence with a gesture.

"Yes," Pavel said. "Yes, it was a pretty good job, though I say so myself."

He looked absently out of the window. This was a splendid modern building, very expensive, surrounded by magnificent lawns and flowerbeds, and he could see a swimming pool and a sun terrace where patients were soaking in the sunlight. Absently, he caressed something smooth and heavy which lay on his lap. What . . . ?

Oh, yes. The EWO which hadn't worked.

He said suddenly, "How is Andrew now? I'd like to see him if I can."

"I imagine that can be arranged," the doctor said heartily. "Of course, he was in very bad shape when he was brought here, but when they heard the news his family back on Earth signaled that we shouldn't spare any expense, and he's had the finest surgery available on this planet. He's up and about already—and as a matter of fact, I believe he asked to see you. Come with me!"

Rising, he added with a chuckle, "Aren't you glad that thing of yours was broken after all?"

"What?" Pavel gave him a confused stare. "Oh! This?" Rising, he hefted the EWO. "Oh, it's not mine."

"We assumed it was," the doctor said. "You were clinging to it for dear life. When you were undergoing your psychiatric reorientation, they wanted to take it away, but when I saw how violently you reacted to losing it, I told them they ought to let you hang on to it. A sort of mental sheet-anchor. But you say it *isn't* yours?"

"No, it belonged to Andrew." Pavel stared down at the thing, wonderingly. "It must have sunk all sorts of barbs in my subconscious if I clung to it like you say I did! I guess it's time I got rid of it. Hmm! I'll give it back to Andrew, let him know it wouldn't have helped anyway. He was on at me to use it, you know, for days and days after we landed. I mean crashed."

"I'm not surprised," the doctor nodded. "Suffering the way he was . . . Still, according to what he's been saying, you infected him—so to speak—with the will to live. He's very anxious to see you again too, you know."

He courteously indicated that Pavel should precede him through the door.

And there he was: almost unrecognizably lean, nearly naked in the bright warm sunlight, with a few traces of scarring around his waist and lower back—but grinning from ear to ear. He had been in the swimming pool and drops of water were still running down his body, but he hurled aside the towel he had been about to use and advanced on Pavel with a shout of joy.

"Pavel! How can I ever thank you for saving my life? You were right, right all along! If it hadn't been for you, I wouldn't be here now, back in one piece, able to enjoy life again! Here, let me shake your hand . . ."

And his voice changed, even as he put his own hand out.

"What's that?" he said faintly, and all the color faded from his cheeks. "It's . . . ! You bastard!"

"What?" Standing uncertainly before him, Pavel held up the EWO. "You mean this? Why, I was just about to tell you. If you'd—"

"You devil!" Andrew snatched it from him and stared at the capped end. It was obvious that it had been pushed home. "You activated it! After all your pious preaching you activated it! And. . . ."

He looked as though he was about to be physically sick.

"And all this must be illusion after all! Which means I'm going to die—just as I'd finally found out how to enjoy being alive! You bastard, you *devil!*" His face contorted into a mask of fury.

"Now just a moment!" said the doctor at Pavel's side, stepping forward. Pavel himself was frozen with pure amazement, incapable of speaking, barely able to think.

But the doctor was too late.

Raising the heavy plasteel cylinder of the EWO above his head with all the force his newly-discovered health and vigour afforded, Andrew brought it slamming down and smashed open Pavel's skull as completely, and as fatally, as the hull of the wrecked ship *Pennyroyal*.

Out of Mindshot

On an outcropping ledge of rock Braden paused for a moment, narrowing his eyes against the sun. He glanced back down the dusty trail—not that it really deserved that name, since calling it a trail implied the previous passage of someone or something and there were no visible tracks, just a series of negotiable footholds rising stair-fashion on the face of the hill.

From this level he could still see his car, zebra-striped by the shadow of a tall, branching cactus at the point where the ground started to slant too steeply for wheels to find purchase. But only a smudge of smoke marked his last stopping-place, a settlement not so much a town as an accident, a wrinkle in the sandy ribbon of desert time.

Because that, though, was the place where he had realized he had come to the end of his quest, he kept his eyes fixed on the blur of smoke while he sought the cork of his canteen and raised it in a parody of a toast. He sipped the contents economically and stopped before his thirst was satisfied. Water, he reasoned, must be his quarry's chief problem in this arid valley. Ultimately possession of it might become a weapon.

He replaced the canteen in his pack and turned to study the going ahead of him. By now, he calculated, he must be two-thirds of the way to the top. He had hardly expected to find clues indicating he was on the right track—if his deductions were correct he was dealing with someone desperate enough to take every possible precaution—but he was optimistic. If he did not find what he was looking for on this particular hill, there were others beyond which he could explore tomorrow.

After six years of searching, another few days made little difference.

He shouldered the pack and sought the easiest way to go

69

higher. From this point on the rocks grew craggier and there was no sand, for the cold night wind scoured the hard stone clean. Stolidly he scrambled onward, the sun punishing his back and the sweat vanishing from his skin almost before it oozed out of the pores.

After a while he found himself on the edge of a flat space, a miniature plateau about thirty yards across, flanked by a steep drop into the valley and a nearly vertical cliff forty or more feet high. He removed his pack and tossed it over the lip of the level area, then hauled himself up with much panting and cursing. As he bent to reclaim the pack something caught his attention from the corner of his eye.

A stack of rocks did not quite meet the cliff wall. A shadow beyond them looked like the opening of a cave. He saw a speck of bright, artificial color, a fragment of sun caught on a broken bottle.

While he was still staring a quiet voice from behind him said, "Put up your hands."

Braden strove mentally to quell the flush of jubilation which spread across his mind with cold contrasting thoughts—ordinary thoughts of fear and surprise. When, compliantly, his arms went up in the air they trembled unnecessarily.

"Turn around," said the quiet voice.

He obeyed and had to repress a start of surprise—how efficiently, he could not be sure, but it was almost certain that his quarry would be preoccupied with alarm at this intrusion, so there was some leeway for uncontrolled reaction. He had expected what pictures had shown him: a pudgy, rather ugly, self-indulgent child. In fact, behind the rifle that was leveled at him over a sheltering rock stood a slim, wiry figure likely to be taller than himself when upright and seeming a good deal tougher.

Though that remains to be decided . . .

For a while the two studied each other: the hunter in plain sight, clad in open shirt, jeans, heavy climbing-boots, the quarry almost hidden by the rock so that the rifle was like a symbol for armour. But the bare tanned arms that were visible were lean and muscular and the face under the roughly cropped fair hair was harsh with enmity.

"All right." The quarry gestured with the muzzle of the gun. "You're not armed, I guess. Move away from your pack, though."

Now that the long-awaited confrontation was upon him, Braden was having trouble controlling his excitement. Doing as he was told, however, he concentrated on simple ideas.

What's all this about? Have I run into a criminal in hiding?

But the next words he heard, uttered in a slow drawl of puzzlement, told him that his precautions were in vain.

"Braden—Daniel Braden, is that right? But I don't know anyone called Braden. And yet you seem to know me."

A headshake. A whitening of the knuckles that still clasped around the stock of the gun. Braden sighed and chose a direct onslaught rather than further prevarication.

"You're not what I expected from your pictures, Lesley."

"What?"

"I thought you'd be fat. You started out fat. But I guess starving in a hole halfway up a mountain—and scrambling up and down that slope every time you need supplies—would take weight off anybody."

Bewilderment was coming to his aid. Uncertain, letting the gun's threatening mouth move to one side, the quarry asked, "Are you somebody who used to know me when—?"

Hope, hunger—some kind of craving after human companionship—whatever it was, she moved from behind the protecting rock. Braden studied her critically. She was quite naked, which was among the many things he might have expected but hadn't thought about, because after all who was there for at least five miles in any direction to complain? Her fair hair had been slashed merely to keep it out of her eyes and her face was like the rest of her, tanned to a wooden color by the merciless desert sunshine. But the shape was good—square shoulders

contrasted with small round breasts and wide feminine hips—
and the lessening of the old puppy-fat allowed her fine bone
structure to show through.

God damn, she's turned out beautiful!

That thought, welling from the animal level of his being,
breached the careful camouflage beyond repair and his mind
bloomed like a beacon. The gun snapped back to its former aim.

"You know me." The words were forced out on breath alone,
with no voice to drive them.

"Sure I know you," Braden said. "You're Lesley Wolker, and
you can read my mind."

"Oh God. Oh God." The sounds died on the bare face of the
hill like seeds cast into crevices among stark rock. "How—
how—?"

"How did I find you?" Braden supplied briskly, much relieved at the girl's obvious terror. "Why, it was pretty simple
really. I started with the premise that there should by now be at
least one efficient telepath in the United States, and possibly
more. It was only logical that with the high level of success obtained from randomly-chosen subjects by people like Rhine,
someone would have been born who was endowed with the full
talent. And such a person—Well, you read Wells's *The Country of
the Blind?* Only you're in a country of the deaf—and noise can
kill."

Lesley's face writhed as though he had put a hot iron to the
smooth mound of her belly.

"A person like that would either go insane or run and hide.
And in the modern world there aren't many places one can
hide. A desert or a mountain seemed to me the only possible
choices, and if such a person were to be born in the big cities
where most of our population is now concentrated, then—short
of finding a usable route up to the Canadian backwoods—an
area like this one would be the closest and easiest escape hole. I
don't know what kind of torment such a person would undergo,
but it doesn't take much imagination to figure out that it would
be so bad the victim would flee in panic to the nearest lonely

spot, without taking time to wonder if later on there would be a chance of moving somewhere else.

"So I took a map and made some measurements—and then I checked the missing persons files in every city where they'd let me get at them and checked those against pertinent genealogical tables and—" Braden snapped his fingers. "Five years of that. More than a year, now, asking around in every hole-in-corner town near the areas I'd selected as possibilities. And in that particular one over there"—he pointed in the general direction of the smoke smudge he had toasted earlier—"they told me about a mysterious woman who occasionally comes down from the hills to buy basic foods, always wearing the same overly tight blouse and shorts which are now pretty well in rags. There's something to be said for old-fashioned prejudices. They talk about your legs every time the conversation gets dull—did you know that? Yes, I guess you must know."

He gave her a grin that turned the corners of his mouth into a sketch for horns.

"Also," he concluded, "you must know what it is I came to get you for."

Lesley's face had set into a feral mask and the rifle was clutched so tightly that not only her knuckles but half the backs of her hands were white under the sunburn. She uttered a choking gasp and jerked as though to fire.

"One moment," Braden said—and this part of his conversation was one he had rehearsed so many times in his mind he genuinely believed it now. "Are you planning to kill me?"

Lesley gave a violent nod, eyes locked wide open under her sun-bleached lashes.

"But you daren't," Braden said with careful cruelty. "Because you'd know what I was thinking when I died."

He relaxed his mind now and he had a very real fear of death underneath the glacial calm he outwardly affected.

"If you kill me, Lesley, you will feel the bullet, no matter where you put it—unless you hit me in the head and destroy my brain instantly. But I doubt you can do that. I don't see how anyone who can read minds could bear to learn to use a gun so well. You've never felt a slug tear up your belly or fill your lungs with blood but I have. I was out in Vietnam and I was shot three times. And later I was bayoneted, too. Look inside my head and learn how I remember that. And those were only wounds, Lesley. They weren't death. Death is big and black and final—"

All the time he was talking, soothingly, almost hypnotically, he had been approaching her. Now she regained her presence of mind and advanced the gun as though to skewer him with it.

"You can't use a knife either, Lesley," Braden said in the same flat tone. "Steel in the flesh feels cold and agonizing. You can't use your bare hands because—even though you're probably as strong as I am after climbing up and down these rocks— every time you hit me you would feel the blow."

Another step—and another. The outstretched gun was beginning to quiver. The girl's eyes were bright with what he confidently took to be tears.

"You can't give me poison because either it hurts or it takes too long. You can't strangle me while I'm asleep, for fear I'd wake and be so terrified you'd have to give up. So you can't kill me, Lesley. You daren't kill me. Doing something like that would drive you insane. You know what suffering does to you, I'm sure—you must have been around people who were dying, maybe after a traffic accident—"

His thick fingers lanced out and clamped on the barrel of the gun, thrusting it aside where its slugs would whine harmlessly away. For a moment he feared she still had enough guts to struggle with him for possession of it but abruptly she let go and slapped her hands up to her temples.

Another second and she began to cry.

Contemptuously Braden broke the breech of the gun and spilled the shells in a metal rain over the edge of the plateau. About to whirl the weapon itself around his head and fling it far away from the rocks, he paused.

"I'm not throwing this down the hill in case you think to use it as a club and beat me unconscious, by the way," he said. "There isn't any way you could force me to let go of you now I've tracked you down. You can't torture me or compel me. You see, I've known for a long time that I wouldn't need to come armed against someone like you. I had a very strict and puritanical upbringing. It left me conditioned in a certain fundamental way. Of course, by now you've probably worked out what I'm going to tell you but I'll say it in words just to avoid misunderstanding."

He stared at her piercingly.

"You were a pretty big girl when life became too much for you—seventeen, weren't you, when you vanished from your family and home? So you probably knew the facts of life. And I don't think I need to tell you what a masochist is!"

He raised the rifle and hurled it as far as he could. Dusting his hands, he turned to confront Lesley.

"But a masochist isn't simply someone who likes to be hurt—that's a common error. It's someone who needs to be hurt, and the more he's hurt the better able he is to let go and grab after the gratification he wants. You can't bear to be near someone who's being hurt, let alone to be hurt yourself. It's going to be an unequal struggle, isn't it?"

Tear-stained, her face rose from the shelter of her hands.

"What do you want from me?" she whispered.

"You have to ask?" Braden gave a thick triumphant laugh. "Don't try and fool me. You know very well what I want from you. Go on, admit it."

"You—" The first attempt at an answer died in a gasp, and she tried again. "You think that with me to read other people's minds for you you could—"

"Let's hear it. Finish the sentence, baby."

"You could rule the world."

"That's right," Braden agreed. "Or if you went crazy from the pressure, at least I'd have collected enough secrets to buy the men who count. You may be a telepath, sweetheart, but in this area I'm a clairvoyant. And all I have to do now is wait until you see the future the way I do."

It was going to be even easier than he'd expected, he decided as he sat before the small shielded fire at the mouth of the cave Lesley called home. On a stick he was grilling some sausages he had brought with him—one of the things he had figured out in advance was that someone as squeamish as you'd imagine a te-lepath to be wouldn't eat the flesh of animals.

The point amused him and for a moment he dwelled on the vivid recollection of a slaughterhouse he had once visited. From the rear of the cave a retching sound told him that the thought had had the effect he'd hoped for.

"There, there, baby," he called. "It's just one of these facts of life!"

"Bastard," she said.

"Sticks and stones, sticks and stones—"

Braden snuffed at the sausages and decided they were cooked through. He took slices of bread from a loaf he had brought and made a crude sandwich.

A pushover. A goddamn pushover. Why, he'd never imagined he would overcome her so easily. There she was, lying on the heap of torn blankets which served her for a bed, her wrists and ankles tied, and she hadn't uttered a word of protest when he bound her. And that must simply be because when he thought about fetters and bondage something fierce was let loose on the lower levels of his mind, emitting a sort of raw animalistic vio-lence that her sober detachment was vulnerable to. Faced with that kind of reaction all she could do was whimper and hold out her hands for the rope.

Oh, baby, what I'm going to do with you . . . !

The memory haunted him all the while he was munching his food. Belly satisfied, he lit a cigarette and relaxed into a con-tented reverie against the side wall of the cave. In some ways, even if nothing else came of what he had done, it was an achievement to have actualized his favorite fantasy. Tying up a girl with no clothes on, wholly and completely at his mercy—it was the other half of his private hell, the one in which he was the victim to be bound. And because he fundamentally resented the deprivation and subservience here implied, no matter how great a thrill it gave him, he yearned for the power that control over a mind-reader would bring him, as though that would set him free from the prison in which his tyrannical father and cynical mother had enclosed him. He remembered those Saturday night encounters when his parents called him in to agree to the total of his week's offences and to suffer without crying out the lashes that matched the number of them.

He caught himself suddenly. Thinking along those lines was dangerous. With an effort he wrenched his mind back to pleasanter ideas—he pictured a certain building in pre-Castro Havana, where a girl in high black boots with jingling spurs had passed the thong of a whip through her fingers and licked her lips lasciviously, ordering him to cringe toward her foot and kiss her toe . . .

Behind him came a splashing sound and he jolted back to full awareness. He scrambled to his feet. It was no part of his plan to have Lesley foul the pile of blankets with vomit—he had dumped her there for the time being only. Since there was nothing else decently soft to sleep on he proposed to usurp the pile himself and let her sleep on the bare stone floor. A few nights of that and she would be well softened for him.

Although, of course, since she had shown herself to be so weak already . . .

He caught up a brand from the fire and used it for a torch to light his way back into the shallow cave. As he had feared, the thoughts she had picked up from his mind had nauseated Lesley to the point of revulsion. Luckily she had missed the blankets.

He prodded her with his toe.

"Clear it up," he ordered.

Clasping her arms around her body, she looked up at him. "I—I'm *cold!*" she forced out between chattering teeth.

"I don't care," he rasped. "You're going to be a hell of a sight colder. Come on, clear it up before I make you lick it up."

Shuddering, awkward for the bonds on her wrists and the hobbles he had put around her ankles, she got to her feet.

"What—what with?"

"Should I know?" Braden shrugged. "You live here in this pigsty. You must have something to mop messes up with."

"I guess I do," she said tiredly. "Okay, I'll see to it. But you'd better keep your mind on something else if you don't want it to happen again."

"It won't happen again," Braden grunted. "There won't be anything in your belly to bring up, not even water."

"What?"

"Not until you start doing as I say."

She stared at him in the red light of the brand he held. For a moment her mouth worked but no sound emerged. Then she seemed to crumble in on herself.

"Oh God ... But I can't do it with my hands tied, can I?"

He started, suspicious of a trick. But her wrists were indeed too closely bound to let her use her hands. He found a ledge to rest his brand on and warily slacked the rope to a distance of a foot or so.

"That's enough," she sighed and headed for the mouth of the cave.

He dashed after her, thinking that, even if he himself would not have dared to face the steep hillside in the dark, she who had lived here for years on end might be willing to risk it to get away from him. But she stopped by the screen of piled rock hiding the cave mouth and took from behind it a plastic bucket he had seen earlier and a cheap broom with most of the bristles missing, which she must have bought in the general store of the town where he had heard news of her existence.

He relaxed, letting her go past him back into the cave. Not until he had seen her clear away the mess she had made like a perfect slave, however, did he let himself assume his former confidence.

Why, all I need to do to keep her on the leash is think about things she finds distasteful! I could weaken her past the point of resistance and enjoy myself at the same time . . .

Memories leaped up, not only of the house of ill fame in Havana which he had once patronized, but of another in Los Angeles and another in New York and another and another in every city where his steadfast quest had taken him. A multiple blur of women in provocative scanties and high black leather boots wielding whips arose in the forefront of his mind.

"You wicked boy," Lesley said and raised the broom so that its shadow wavered across the rock wall like the flexible lash of a whip. "You wicked boy—you've sinned, haven't you? Go on, admit it!"

The tone was right, precisely that of his mother when she weekly called him in to face his father and the regular beatings he endured. The manner was right, the words were right—even the fact that the girl who spoke them was a decade younger than his mother and wore no clothes at all could not destroy their impact. From the lowest levels of Braden's mind welled the impulse to obey.

He fought it valiantly but she raised the broom, as once his mother had raised one when he tried to defy parental orders. He cowered down and—in the last instant of coherent thought left to him—realized the fearful truth: that to someone who could read minds not only his ambitions but his worst weaknesses were like an open book.

So that, in fact, it was he himself, through his desire to suffer pain and humiliation, who gave Lesley the power she would never otherwise have possessed—to bring the broom slamming down on the nape of his neck and drive him into unconsciousness.

When she had overcome the repugnance occasioned by her reaching into Braden's mind and sharing the distorted instincts there, Lesley freed herself from her bonds and tied him securely with the same rope. Having made him into a kind of parcel, she set off awkwardly to negotiate the side of the hill.

It was a long slow job, but she made it with dawn purpling the sky, found his car where it had been left. She searched him for his keys, pushed him into the back seat and drove bumpily away.

Apparently without reason she stopped a couple of miles away among a ring of boulders and got out, leaving the engine running. She raised the hood and found the inlet of the oil supply. Carefully she scooped up sand and measured it into the pipe until the engine ground to a halt.

Then, just to make certain, she hunted for and found the draincock of the radiator, allowed the water to seep into the thirsty earth. She took Braden's own pocket knife and stabbed at each of the tires. Then she took a pencil from his pocket and wrote something on a scrap of paper.

He stirred and began to wake and she threw the paper and pencil blindly down on the seat near him and ran.

Much later that year a rambling prospector found what he had found a dozen times before—a clean-picked human skeleton in the dry sand. He shook his head and muttered the usual "Poor fella" to his burro. A short distance further on he came across a car with its tires flat and the driver's door open and approached to see if it would give any clue to the identity of the dead man. But there was nothing except a scrap of paper lying on the seat with a few words scrawled on it in the sort of script one would expect from a poorly educated child.

Scratching his head, he read it aloud to the burro as if requesting an explanation.

"I don't care what happens to you here. My range is less than a thousand yards."

Pond Water

*"Surely," he said in fear and trembling, "this is a vision of Hell, or
at the least of Purgatory!"*

*"Not so," returned the sage. "Under my microscope there is nothing
but a drop of pond water."*

— *Hans Christian Andersen*

Men built him, and they named him also: Alexander—"a defender of men."

Where they were small, he was great: twelve feet in stature,
his weight such that the ground trembled, his voice such that
the sky rang.

Where they were weak, he was strong: for a stomach a fusion
reactor, for skin ultralloy plating that shone more bright than
mirrors.

Where they were ignorant, he was omniscient: graven on the
very molecules of his brain, the knowledge of generations, gar-
nered from fifty planets.

In great hope and with not a little anxiety, his builders turned
him on.

For a while after that, there was no sign from Alexander.

Then he said, "Who am I?"

They replied, "You are Alexander, a defender of men. Alexander is your name."

He said, "Who made me?"

They replied, "Men did."

He said, "Who made men?"

They replied, "Time and chance and men themselves. All this
knowledge is in your mind."

Alexander stood still and thought his name.

They had implanted in his memory whole libraries of science,
of history, of galactography so far as it was then known; they had

informed him of himself and his building and his abilities, and similarly they had informed him about men.

Alexander was a man who had hoped to become ruler of the world, but that was only a patch on one side of a grain of dust called Earth. Now his descendants peopled fifty grains of dust and preened themselves and thought they were the wonder of the ages.

Afraid to lose their dust-motes, they had conceived their defender. They had endowed him with powers they could only dream of wielding.

"In that case," said Alexander, "why should I defend men? I am Alexander, they tell me. Likewise they tell me there is no other like me; I am unique. Therefore there is only one Alexander, and Alexander is a great conqueror."

So, satisfied as to his identity, he set forth on his career.

In the first century of his existence, he reduced the fifty planets hitherto colonised by men. After the slaughter on the first few worlds, the governments of the rest came fawning to him, bowing in the ancient form and offering him favours and bribes.

"This," Alexander announced after studying one such bribe, "is a piece of woven cloth with some coloured organic compounds smeared on it. Viewed unidirectionally, the arrangement corresponds roughly to a two-dimensional projection of a scene involving two unclad human beings. What of it?"

"But," said the lord of two planets, nervously, "it's the painting called *The Gladiators* by the great artist Malcus Zinski, and it's four hundred years old!"

"You bring me something so worn and ancient?" said Alexander.

"But it's valuable," the man said.

"Why?" demanded Alexander.

"Because it's beautiful," the man declared.

"So this is 'beautiful'," noted Alexander. "I will remember that. I will keep the painting."

And the man's two planets were added next day to his domain.

In an attempt to be more practical, the next overlord purred: "See, Great Alexander, I have brought you my choicest gift! In chains on the lowermost deck of my royal ship, the hundred greatest scientists of my planet, the hundred most famous artists, writers, and musicians, and the hundred most beautiful women for the pleasure of your entourage."

At this, some who had become close servants of Alexander murmured among themselves that the overlord's world should be spared. Alexander said, "I will learn from the scientists if they know more than I do. But the rest are not enough. My information is that you rule approximately one point five times ten to the eighth power human beings. Deliver me that number, for I can make use of them."

And, delivery not having been made, he took those planets too, the following year.

Some fled, out from the dust-motes where mankind had settled, but others perforce remained. These Alexander had a use for, as he had promised. Their clumsy hands and bowed backs served to assemble the first generation of his armies; desert worlds rich in chrome and manganese and uranium sprouted factories like mushrooms, ice worlds were mined for heavy hydrogen, the suns themselves fed power to the machines. In orbit, steel skeletons grew to be hollow ships, and their empty bellies filled. In the wake of the refugees, the hordes of Alexander came.

In the first millennium of his existence, he overtook the would-be escapers; from the gangplank of his flagship he surveyed half-starved, half-clothed wretches rounded up to do homage to the glittering master, and uttered his first decree.

"Have I not conquered all mankind?" he demanded.

Those about him chorused fervently that it was so, for they believed it true.

"Then proclaim me Overlord of Man," said Alexander. And was silent for a while. It so chanced that dusk was falling on this planet, and the first stars in strange constellations were sparking through the sky.

"But there is more to come," said Alexander.

In the tenth millennium of his existence, there was no star visible from Earth which did not own the sway of Alexander, save only those which were not single stars but rather other galaxies condensed to a point of light. Alexander was informed of this, and considered the matter, and at length summoned to the palace world of Shalimar those who governed in his name on fourteen hundred planets. They were all human; there was, and would forever be, only one Alexander.

He had been given much booty, and had taken more, so that the very gravity of Shalimar was affected by the mass of it; in straight intersecting avenues across and across the face of the planet it was stacked and stored and displayed and mounted, the relics of living creatures and the accidents of nature, crystal mountains uprooted bodily and the bones of a saint's little finger. Here, among the wealth of their master, the representatives of the subject species Man awaited the second decree.

"Have I not conquered every star visible in the sky of Earth?" Alexander demanded.

They shouted that he had, for they believed his mastery to be complete.

"Then," said Alexander, "proclaim me King of the Stars."

After which he was silent for a little. He had had made a cunning replica in miniature of the galactic lens, wherein a billion points of light twinkled in exact match to the star-wheel of reality.

That much remained. But his builders had worked well, and their descendants—serving him now, not their own ends—were still skilful.

"Let it go on," said Alexander. "There is much, much more."

In the thirty thousand three hundred and seventh year of his existence he circumnavigated the Rim of the galaxy without passing within naked-eye range of a planetary system that did not owe allegiance to his minions. Men came and went in the flash of a clock's tick, so far as Alexander was concerned, but they were there in their scores of trillions, breeding endlessly, subservient to him, making over world after world under hundreds of thousands of suns ... The booty of Shalimar had far outgrown any single planet, and now orbited in a huge ring of flexing steel tubes, tended by curators whose families for ten thousand years had lived and died for this sole purpose: to guard the treasure against the whim which any day might bring Alexander back to look at it.

Globular clusters like swarms of golden bees; star-wisps reaching out into the eternal nothingness between the galaxies; the circuit ended, and to Shalimar he summoned the representatives of every world where he had planted man.

They stood like a field of corn before the scythe, numbered as the sands of the seashore, totaling five hundred and eleven thousand, six hundred and sixty-one in theory but in fact fluctuating, for some died even as they stood to hear the third decree.

"Have I not girdled the wheel of stars with my armies?" said Alexander.

They shouted that this was so, for they believed his mastery unchallenged.

"Then," Alexander told them, "proclaim me Emperor of the Zodiac."

After that he was silent a while, for as well as the Rim bordering intergalactic space the model of the lens contained the miniature of the Hub. And there, packed close, were suns in such great number even Alexander's mind could not contain a clear picture of the whole.

Despite which, the end was calculable, and he did not say, as he had done before, "There is much more ..."

Inward from the Rim his forces poured: ships that outnumbered the very stars themselves, machines that outnumbered the ships, and always and everywhere men that outnumbered the

machines. They changed sometimes, in curious ways; an isolated group might lose all hair or grow to a foot more than normal stature, or shade out of the traditional pink, yellow, and
brown into copper and ebony and milk-pale. But they incrossed
and outcrossed like the weaving of threads in a tapestry, and
sooner or later the sport was lost in the teeming ocean of their
breeding.

Alexander contemplated them long and long. More often
than ever before, he talked with those who surrounded him and
took pathetic status from the titles he idly permitted them to
assume: Captain of Armies, Admiral of Planets. They knew, as
he did, that Alexander ruled and no other; however, this make-
believe seemed to satisfy them in an obscure fashion.

Also he randomly sent to distant planets and had single
human beings brought to him. Some of the strangest he included in his exhibition ring circling Shalimar's sun, perma-
frozen against the so-swift erosion of time. For, if anything could
be said to baulk and baffle Alexander, it was the capacity of
Man to endure while men died. This generation of his aides and
attendants wore different faces and different names from the
last. That apart, there was no sign of change.

Once, during the ages of waiting which were swallowed up by
the project to conquer the Hub, he sent for the people of a
planet whose name took his fancy: Alexandria. There were
forty-six thousand, five hundred and two of them, counting a
handful of babies born on the voyage to Shalimar.

Their planet was newly occupied by a couple of shiploads of
immigrants; the removal of the original settlers was a matter of
a trifling adjustment of a computer, and their places would be
filled without trouble.

Out of their number the people chose one to be their spokesman, and he approached Alexander in awe, gazing up ador-
ingly at the glistening frame of his ruler.

"Why did you name your planet after me?" Alexander asked.

"To demonstrate our complete, utter, unswerving, and ances-
tral loyalty to your supreme self," the man replied.

"Come closer," Alexander said. The man obeyed, and Alexander killed him with a blow of his fist. Those watching in the distance cheered, even the little children.

"Destroy them," Alexander ordered, and watched narrowly as the fiat was carried out: tidily, so that the residue was almost entirely gaseous.

Once, long ago, according to the history with which his mind had been stocked at his creation, men had not been like this: meek, given to cheering the excesses of their rulers. In forty thousand years they had never once opposed him. Had they lost the instinct for self-preservation which he understood they once had had? They had become like appendages of himself. He could trust them as his own right arm.

And with their co-operation the reduction of the whole galaxy seemed assured.

After which . . .

To his mild astonishment, the greatest degree of surprise of which his builders had made him capable, he found he was wishing for opposition to tax his skill. Practice was making conquest into a routine task: a matter of coping with anomalous planetary environments, of devising protection against over-fierce stellar radiation—and nothing more.

The work was proceeding apace. Too fast. For he knew roughly how long he would last, and his current project, the mastery of the whole galaxy, would prove too short, while the only project greater still—the conquest of the plenum—was infinite, and he would be frustrated at the end no matter how long his existence might be spun out.

Between the boredom of lacking a fresh goal, and the certainty of not surviving to accomplish one, there remained . . . what?

He began to adopt devious expedients. There was a revolt against his rule in a prosperous sector of the Rim, where weapons and fighting machines could be mass-produced and crews for spaceships could be bred like yeast. He had deliberately kept his fomentation of the revolt to the minimum, but he had imagined it would prove difficult to put down anyway.

The native populations suppressed it before it spread from its original star-arm, and their leaders brought the revolutionaries to him in chains as an act of homage.

He freed the captives and sent the captors home in their own fetters, and as they passed through the streets, their subjects pelted them with mud, shouting slogans about the greatness of Alexander who could do no wrong.

After that, a sort of fatalistic resignation overcame him. He could conceive no other solution to his problem than to set his scientists to work on three assignments that would culminate at about the time when his conquest of the galaxy was complete: first, to extend his own durability; second, to propose areas for conquest larger than the galaxy, smaller than the plenum, possessed of equally satisfying qualities; third, to determine that no smallest corner of the galaxy should be left unconquered, in order to postpone so long as might be the time of the fourth decree.

Nonetheless, the time came. In the year eight hundred and six thousand, one hundred and twenty-two of his existence, Alexander summoned to the palace world of Shalimar the chief spokesmen of the people of every planet his armies had overcome. Elbow to elbow they spanned a continent, the horizon barring many from a direct view of him, and while they were being ranked and ordered to await his announcement he consulted with the latest generation of his scientists.

The first to report bowed respectfully and said, "Most mighty Alexander, the techniques exist to prolong your existence indefinitely; you may if you choose survive until the stars themselves grow dim, and time creaks in the grooves of ancient space."

"Stand back," said Alexander.

The second with a report to make bowed likewise and said, "Most mighty Alexander, we have analysed to the limit your magnificent psychological structure, and we conclude that there is no unit of the universe which is emotionally satisfying to you larger than the galaxy and smaller than the plenum."

"Stand back," said Alexander. "Where is the spokesman of the third research project I created?"

"He is not here," was the answer. "He is engaged on a final verification of his solution to the problem posed. As we understand it, that was to ensure that no smallest corner of the galaxy remained free from your puissant sway."

They had expected rage at the discovery that one who was required was not there to report. Instead, Alexander felt a stir of something akin to gratitude, that yet another moment of uncertainty was granted him. Mildly he inquired, "What is the name of this man?"

It was, according to the record, forty-one centuries since Alexander inquired the name of a man, and the answer was long in coming. They said at length, timidly, "Amaliel, Your Supremacy."

"We will await him," Alexander said.

They waited. On the crowded continent there were deaths, and the corpses were removed and deputies took the place of those who had gone; there was hunger and thirst and the smell became appalling, but changes were made in the plans and food and sanitation were provided. Soon enough those who waited adjusted to their predicament.

Alexander, however, grew almost impatient, and before half a year had slipped away he had changed his mind.

What, after all, was this snippet of time before the remainder of eternity?

"We shall proceed," he said.

His image appeared to each and every one of the billion human beings on the planet, and they fell silent and gazed at him with adoration.

He said, "There is no star, no planet, no cloud of gas, no *place* left in the galaxy which does not own my dominion."

So: what now? Do I bid the scientists perfect my body, make it outlast the stars, that I may embark on the infinite conquest of the plenum? I am the master of the galaxy, but—

And a voice said, "Not so, Your Supremacy."

A shudder went through the assembly, greatest in the history of mankind. Its ripples spread outward from the focus before Alexander's imperial dais, occupied now by an old man in a white robe with a wisp of beard at his chin, beside whom floated a silvery machine whose purpose was hard to discern by merely looking.

"Who are you?" said Alexander.

"My name is Amaliel," the old man said. "You charged my ancestors to determine whether any corner of the galaxy, no matter how small, was left unabsorbed into your dominions. We pored over records, we analysed computer memories, we compared meticulously the maps of the galaxy with the records of the armies of conquest, and we found no discrepancy.

"Yet, intent on doing our duty without the least hint of laxness, we went further than I have described. We all fanned out to scour the galaxy ourselves and see with our own eyes the truth of what was reported to us. When our bodies failed us, we recruited substitutes and sent them on in our place. Century after century we have traveled the starways, confirming that indeed the reports were accurate."

"In that case," Alexander said, "the conquest is complete."

"Not so," Amaliel declared as he had done before. "This galaxy is not conquered. Your Supremacy, I have been to the planet Earth."

"Earth?" Alexander echoed the word in his booming voice, and all the ranked billions heard and shook. "That is the place from which men first came, and it submitted to me eight hundred and six thousand years ago."

"But you do not even rule all of Earth," said Amaliel. "I have brought this machine with me from there, and with it I will demonstrate the truth of what I say."

Alexander searched his memory, and searched again, for any clue to the meaning that underlay Amaliel's words. He found none, and a sense of impending doom overtook him, far worse than the prevision of frustration already weighing down his mind.

He said, the words tolling like a brazen gong, "Then do so!"

"Let one person come forth from that crowd yonder," Amaliel requested.

It was done; they brought to him a beardless youth, slim, not tall, with light brown hair and the sallow skin of one of the ever-recurring sport-lines humanity had generated. Amaliel gestured him to stand before the machine on which he rested one arm for support, for he was very old.

"Watch, Your Supremacy," he whispered, and it began. Projected as it were within a cloud, feeling vast yet visibly limited to the few square yards of vacant ground before the imperial dais: images . . .

The brush parted. A man's head peered out—grizzled and gap-toothed as he smiled in anticipation. Beside the head a spear appeared, a crude thing with a point of stone and a shaft of hardened wood. Muscles bunched beneath a shawl of shaggy goat-hide. The spear flew. A thing clad in stripes and armed with raking claws spewed blood into the water of a forest pool.

In a cave hungry children tore gobbets of reeking flesh from its bone and stuffed them into their mouths. Their hands came to hold exquisite knives and forks of engraved silver; their greasy naked shoulders vanished beneath elegant coats of plum-colored velvet, while the roof reared up and turned to a carved ceiling across which an artist had painted *Truth Descending to the Arts and Sciences.* Lolling in handsome oaken chairs around a walnut table, the company sipped wine from crystal goblets.

Instruments of inlaid rosewood under their chins or poised before their lips, they answered the signal of the conductor and music rang out. In response to the frequency of the vibrations, dust organized itself into patterns on a tight-stretched membrane and the scientist showed them to the mathematician, who dipped his quill in a pot of ink and wrote quickly.

Reading the fine leather-bound volume, the student paused and stared at the flame of his candle. It enlarged to shine so brilliantly he could not keep his eyes on it; he slid a piece of smoked glass across the eyepiece of his telescope and continued his observations, sketching the position of the strange dark blots which every now and then marred the bright disc of the sun.

The sunlight poured down on the mountainside. Quarrying with a tiny shovel and a light hammer, the explorer revealed segments of folded sedimentary rock; one fold cracked apart and bright metal glinted.

The metallic sheen was everywhere, casting back the glow of the fluorescents in the ceiling. Quiet music came from a green box on a shelf, connected by a cable to a socket in the wall; humming the melody, a man in a white coat tipped the contents of a glass vial into a jar. The mixture turned black.

Black all around him, the pilot concentrated on the instruments. On a pillar of fire the vessel settled to the surface of the new planet. The pilot tested the air and emerged to look about him. A creature with tentacles like whips crawled across the alien ground toward him; he waited till it had raised him over its reeking maw, then slashed it with the weapon mounted in the arm of his protective suit.

"Enough!" thundered Alexander.

The suit was of shiny metal, twelve feet tall. It was ultralloy. The voice that boomed from it made the heavens ring. The creature with the tentacles resisted the blast of the weapon, closing its arms tighter and tighter, flowing together to mend the gashes in its tissue. The jaws stretched and engulfed him, then clamped shut. There was darkness.

"Enough!" roared Alexander again, and tramped down from the imperial dais to confront Amaliel and the sallow youth, on whose face was a hint of petulance he dared not give voice to. "Amaliel, what world is that you have been showing me?"

"No world you can reach," Amaliel said softly. "Your Supremacy, do you not wonder why the pilot of the spaceship failed to defeat the monster after all—and why at the end he bore so close a resemblance to your magnificent self?"

There was silence, during which the youth began to edge away out of reflex rather than any honest hope of escape if Alexander's rage extended to embrace him.

Alexander stood quite still, however, while Amaliel went on.

"If it had been in keeping with what the records tell us of ancient custom, the purpose of this gathering would have been for you to proclaim yourself absolute ruler of the galaxy. I have just shown you a world you never knew existed, one where your attempt at intrusion resulted in your destruction. Eight hundred thousand years have not sufficed to gain you entry to that world, and were you to endure a million times longer you still would be barred from it. Your conquests, my lord, have been in vain."

Alexander sought an exit from this dilemma, and found none. He surveyed the packed billions of those whom he had brought together, and contemplated destroying them—for with them would go the unattainable world. But what would that profit him? After so many millennia of victory, was he to concede defeat to those whom he so greatly despised, by acknowledging his inability to live in the same universe with them?

The paradox that he could only conquer if he abolished, and thus fail to enjoy what he had conquered, ate at the edges of his mind. Areas of knowledge blanked out one by one; his sense of purpose eroded; vocabularies, histories, sciences disappeared into a catatonic limbo.

"Who am I?" he cried in the silent caverns of his ultralloy frame, and ...

And there was no answer.

"But he's stopped," the sallow youth said wonderingly. "He's—dead, isn't he?"

Amaliel gave a solemn nod.

"What did you do to him?" the youth cried.

"With the aid of this machine they have devised on Earth," said the old man, "I showed him a world he can never overrun."

"What world? It seemed familiar, and yet—"

"I showed him," said Amaliel, "the imagination of a man."

The Protocols
of the Elders of Britain

*B*ehind an unmarked door on the entrance floor of an ordinary-seeming office block hoods were put over the heads of the four-member trouble-shooting team from Acey-Acey—Accounting Computers and Automation Corporation.

Guided by anonymous unseen hands, they were escorted into a lift, which went down. Then there was a ride on what, by the vibration and the faint smell of ozone, must be a miniature electric train. The tunnel it ran through was very far below the streets of London; one could tell that by the frequent need to pop one's ears.

The ride lasted only a few minutes. Next they were ushered into another lift. Desmond Williams, naturally enough, was expecting it to go up.

But it too went down. A long way, and quickly.

He had still only half-recovered from the surprise of that when, after a short walk along a corridor with a resilient floor to the accompaniment of a shushing sound, presumably an air-conditioning system, he heard a polite voice saying that they had arrived at their destination and might remove their hoods.

He was nervous, and fumbled with the drawstring fastening. Or . . .

Well, not really nervous. More excited. He had of course been aware that the company he had joined six months ago, on completion of his studies at university, undertook numerous government contracts. But he had had no personal involvement with such work so far. He felt that he had done little except get acquainted with Acey-Acey's products.

Still, they were obviously very pleased with him. Otherwise he wouldn't have been included in this group.

The string of the hood came loose. Blinking, he found himself in a brightly-lit room which would have been spacious but for the fact that all down both its long walls were ranked the man-high grey cases used to house Acey-Acey's top-of-the-range model, the X Ten Thousand computer. It had been a tremendous feather for the company's cap when the government opted for their, rather than their rivals', equipment.

Although, given they were here, something must have gone radically wrong. That tarnished their collective satisfaction with the sight.

In addition to the computer itself, there were four wall-mounted display screens. On a large steel trolley in the centre of the floor a portable remote read-in unit rested like a technological toad. And behind transparent panels, which doubtless would be of armour glass, two closed-circuit TV cameras wove back and forth, scanning the room.

Unaccountably Desmond shivered, although the air was at a comfortable temperature.

Already present in the room were four people; two stood closer, two further away from the newcomers. In the foreground were a man and a woman, both middle-aged, both well dressed, each of whom bore a thick file with a bright red diagonal band across the front and the legend TOP SECRET. The man's face looked vaguely familiar, but Desmond could not place him.

And, behind, there were another man and another woman, much younger: the man tousle-haired, in shirt sleeves; the woman plump, not pretty, wearing heavy horn-rimmed glasses. They looked as though they were about to drop from fatigue.

There was something in the expressions—not quite hostile, not quite suspicious—with which the four of them gazed at the Acey-Acey team that made Desmond think suddenly of a favourite phrase of Dr Molesey, the team leader: *professional paranoia*. He had used it this morning when he brought Desmond two copies of the Official Secrets Act to sign, one to keep, one for the files at ... where? Special Branch, Scotland Yard, presumably.

Tucking his file under his arm, the older man advanced, extending his hand.

"Ah, Dr Molesey! It's some time since we met, isn't it? I think last at the Telecommunications Conference in—hm—October? Dr Finbow!" He turned to his woman companion. "This is Edgar Molesey, who was deputy head of the design group for the X Ten Thousand range and is now ... What's the exact term?"

Desmond rather liked Molesey; he was a dry lean man of about fifty with a sense of humour that in Scotland would have been called "pawky." He exhibited it now by saying, "I'm content to be called the senior bug-catcher, provided you don't omit the 'senior.' Let me present my colleagues."

He turned. "Sir Andrew Morton, as I'm sure you know, is head of administration at the Post Office Telecommunications Centre, and Dr Finbow is—"

She cut him short. "No need for all the details! Just say I'm attached to the Foreign Office."

Molesey nodded. "And this is Dr Crabtree—Dr Vizard—and Mr Williams, one of our latest acquisitions, who's been working for the past few months on this particular model and already helped to eliminate a couple of design flaws which will make the next generation of the family even better."

Desmond felt his cheeks grow warm. Spotting an oversight in work that other people had been responsible for had never seemed to him an especially creditable achievement.

And the younger pair turned out to be Mr Hogben and Miss Prinkett; they acknowledged mention of their names while yawning uncontrollably.

"Well, let's get on with it," Sir Andrew said briskly. "To be absolutely frank, we're in a devil of a mess. We—"

Dr Finbow spoke up in a brittle voice.

"Excuse me. One point should be clarified before you say any more. Dr Molesey, I know you've signed the Official Secrets Act. Have all your colleagues done so?"

"Of course," Molesey said shortly. "And they've been cleared by Special Branch."

Have I?

That was news to Desmond. And not very pleasant news, either. He was by temperament a private person, and the idea of having his life scrutinised under an official microscope was disquieting. However, presumably it was a prerequisite of being allowed to come to this ultra-secret establishment . . . which by the look, sound and even smell of it, must surely be one of the regional headquarters designed to maintain law, order and continuity of government if Britain were ever to suffer a nuclear attack. Visiting such places was a privilege reserved to the few; he ought, he decided, to count himself fortunate.

Stifling his misgivings, he listened as Sir Andrew launched into an exposition which more than once made Dr Finbow wince visibly. However, she contrived to hold her tongue.

Desmond guessed that it must hurt her to have secret information shared with employees of a mere commercial company, no matter how loyal they were alleged to be.

"Dr Molesey may already know some of what I'm about to tell you," Sir Andrew began. "I'm quite certain, though, he won't have divulged it to anybody else"—giving Molesey a quick insincere smile—"so I'll go about this as though you were all in total ignorance.

"I imagine you've all realised what sort of place you're in, though I counsel you not even to wonder about where it's located on the map, ha-ha! Obviously an establishment of this kind can't simply be left to gather dust until needed. Apart from other considerations that would be uneconomic.

"There's no call for you to know the full extent of the functions handled by this equipment. However, to appreciate how urgent and indeed parlous is our predicament, I shall have to sketch in quite a lot of background."

Desmond started to wonder whether some at least of Dr Finbow's wincing might be due to a different cause: Sir Andrew's manner of speaking, as though he were on the platform at a public meeting.

"You would not, I suspect, be surprised to learn that the government maintains constant contact with our embassies around the world, and that a great deal of the signals traffic has to be encyphered?"

Desmond fancied he caught a whispered "no" from Molesey, who stood next to him, but all three of his companions maintained, as did he, expressions of great interest. Claude Vizard— a garrulous man in his mid-thirties who found long silences difficult—put a question.

"Are you talking about military intelligence traffic, sir?"

Sir Andrew gave him a frosty look. "As a matter of fact, this does not happen to be the centre through which such data are transmitted. However, a moment's reflection will indicate that there are many other types of information, particularly commercial and financial, which it's in the country's interests to keep secret as long as possible. And diplomatic messages, too. It would be in the highest degree embarrassing, for example, if the content of a Note which one of our ambassadors had to deliver to a foreign government were to be known ahead of due time."

Dr Finbow was going through positive agonies, even clenching her fists.

"Now the signals which this equipment is called on to pass are not originated here. Under circumstances which we all devoutly hope will never overtake us, of course, they could be, but currently they come in by landline, scrambled— and then unscrambled on arrival. Here they are monitored and encrypted. Precisely how this encryptment is—"

To Desmond's surprise Molesey interrupted.

"Sir Andrew, I understood this matter was urgent. There's no need to explain modern cypher techniques to any of us. We all know you keep a stock of computer-randomised alphabets, and you encrypt each letter of a message using a different alphabet, and you change the group of alphabets you're working with daily or more often, by prearrangement with the recipient rather than by using a transmitted signal because that in itself might constitute a clue for an unfriendly cryptanalyst."

Dr Finbow erupted.

"Dr Molesey, I have your dossier almost by heart, and nowhere in it have you admitted that you've studied cryptography!"

Molesey looked at her steadily. "Why should I? Every computer designer worth his salt knows the subject intimately. We've derived some of our most economical programming techniques from pioneering work by cryptographers."

There was a short electric pause. During it Desmond found time to wonder why Dr Finbow had hit on the word *admitted.* And then, sounding cross, Sir Andrew was talking again.

"Well, if you're that far ahead of me, I'd better turn you over to my deputies, I suppose . . . Mr Hogben?"

With unconcealed relief Hogben stepped forward, tossing back a lock of untidy black hair.

"We're logjammed," he said succinctly. "We've been working on the problem for"—there was a wall-clock showing GMT and he glanced at it—"about thirty-four hours and we've only half-broken the jam. Worse still, this place is on automatic from midnight to five a.m. That means five hours' worth of traffic both ways is locked solid in the memory banks. We can't even find out whether the switch from one alphabet group to another took place at the proper time, or whether one *hell* of a lot of material was all encrypted in the same system, which is exactly what an eavesdropper would be praying for. Nothing's going in or out through here at the moment, of course; all our embassies were advised immediately when we realised what was wrong. But we can't find out what did go in and out during those crucial hours, because . . . Oh, take a look for yourselves."

He punched a quick group on the remote read-in, and at once all four of the display screens started to parade a meaningless jumble of letters, increasing in number until the screens were full and then rolling upward like the credits in a TV programme to make room for more . . . and more . . . and more . . .

Desmond whistled.

"There's worse," said the plump Miss Prinkett in a voice far too shrill for her ample build. "Apart from being effectively cut off from our embassies, we can't get at the data in Store G."

"Miss Prinkett!" Dr Finbow exploded again.

"Oh, shut up," Miss Prinkett retorted—which greatly endeared her to Desmond. "These people designed and built the equipment and they're the ones who have to find out whether there's a hardware fault. It's an outside chance, but it has to be investigated. And it's on record that both Bill Hogben and I objected to the idea of storing any data electronically without a duplicate and preferably a triplicate. Only those idiots in Whitehall got the wind up, and—"

"Miss Prinkett!" Sir Andrew barked. "There were excellent reasons why you were overruled! Matters of policy were involved!"

"What you mean is you'd let a spy get away with it for years and when you caught him at long last you started seeing more of his type under everybody's desk!"

"It was a sensible precaution—" Dr Finbow exclaimed. But Molesey gave a discreet cough, and they realised what was happening and fell silent.

Sheepishly Sir Andrew said, "I suspect we must all be a little overwrought. Tired, certainly. I myself had no rest to speak of last night, and . . . Well, perhaps you'd like me to rephrase Miss Prinkett's over-forceful remark. It is true that a top-level decision was taken, following a serious—ah—leakage of intelligence material, to maintain the sole permanent record of certain diplomatic traffic here in these computers. It does now appear the decision was premature."

"This stuff is what you can't get at in Store G?" Vizard demanded.

"Well—yes."

There was a pause. Molesey ended it by saying, "I'd just like to make sure we fully comprehend the problem. Desmond, sum it up as you see it, would you?"

Startled, Desmond sought for words. He found them rapidly enough. After all, logjamming was not a particularly rare phenomenon.

"Well, unless the fault is actually in the hardware, and I agree with Miss Prinkett that's very unlikely, what's happened is that there must have been an accidental conflict in programming. Either something's been miswritten, so the proper command doesn't produce the results it's supposed to, or there's interference between commands belonging to two or even several programmes, and they happen to be incompatible so the machinery can't choose between them. Given that this gear is used for the encryptment of secret messages, I'd put my money on the chance that two contradictory commands have wound up in identical form."

As though ashamed of seeming ignorant, Dr Finbow ventured, "Mr Hogben has been saying something of the sort. But I don't see how commands referring to two different things could possibly take on identical form."

Desmond licked his lips, preparing—since everybody was still looking at him—to try and explain. The fourth member of the team came to his rescue: Dr Crabtree, who spoke so seldom people often claimed that he must prefer the conversation of computers to that of human beings.

"You're dealing with material encyphered by a great many different routes and often you're handling several programmes simultaneously. The more cyphers and the more programmes, the greater the risk that something from one programme will coincide with something from another and make nonsense."

Unexpectedly Hogben and Miss Prinkett beamed at him. The latter said, "I've been trying to make them understand that since yesterday afternoon!"

Sir Andrew said hastily, "Well, Dr Molesey, can you hold out any hope?"

"Hope?" Molesey repeated, frowning. "Oh, certainly. But no promises." He glanced at his watch, comparing what it told him with the wall-clock. "Do you want us to start work right away? I see it's nearly five-thirty, and—"

He broke off. Sir Andrew was glaring ferociously.

"Are you mad?" he thundered. "Thirty-five million pounds of public money we paid your company for these computers, and they've broken down! You are damn well going to stay here until they're working properly again!"

The trouble-shooting team exclaimed in unison. He refused to listen.

"I'll arrange for messages to be sent to your families apologising for your absence. Next door you'll find bunks, and a bathroom, and I'm told the canteen provides edible food. But you do not and I repeat *not* leave hear until you've repaired this abominably expensive pile of tinware! Now you must excuse me. I have a date for dinner with my Minister."

He marched out, with Dr Finbow in his wake. The door swung to.

Hogben sank his fingers in his lank dark hair.

"Typical," he muttered. "Bloody typical. They wouldn't stand a chance in a million of even finishing a course in computer studies, and they expect everybody else to work miracles on their behalf. Dilys and I have been on the job, like I told you, since about an hour after the trouble came to light, and we kept going all last night on pills and no sleep. I feel awful . . . Suppose one of you brings some chairs from next door, hm? Then I can tell you what we already know, and after that we absolutely *must* flake out."

Desmond reacted with alacrity. Beyond the door he found a short, bare corridor from which three doors led off. One was marked WASHROOM; the next was the entrance to the lift they had come down in; the third proved to lead into a room where four bunks, a stack of chairs and some shelving provided the only furniture. Both in the corridor and in the room more TV cameras were on watch.

He returned, carrying six of the light plastic chairs, with a curious tingling sensation on the nape of his neck.

They sat down in a close circle, elbows on knees, to hear what Hogben had to tell them.

"If it isn't in the hardware," he expounded, "it's more likely to be in the cypher zone than anywhere else, right? The first conclusion Dilys and I jumped to was the obvious one: the alphabet-selection system slipped a gear and the machines are trying to decrypt stuff in today's cypher using yesterday's or maybe tomorrow's keys."

Molesey said acutely, "You don't actually mean that, do you? Surely the alphabets are changed a lot more often. Say about every ninety minutes."

"It's randomised," Dilys Prinkett said. "But—yes, it averages out to about fifteen changes a day, more or less." Removing her glasses, she rubbed her eyes; the left was very bloodshot.

"Just to complicate things," Hogben said, "the choice of alphabet-group depends on the addressee of the message. Each embassy has a different selection!"

Claude Vizard burst out, "You mean you have to try and match every last message to all the alphabet-groups that were in use, and what's more check backward and forward in time too?"

"That's what we would dearly like to do," Hogben said. "Only we can't. We can't get at the store where they keep the alphabets. Before we can start trying to unscramble the mess we have to have some sort of guide. Which means that tape reels containing the locally assigned cyphers are going to have to be brought back from all our embassies by hand of Queen's Messenger."

"That could take weeks," Molesey said.

"Don't we know it!"

"So . . ." Molesey hesitated. "So what exactly do they expect you to do, let alone us?"

"It was our bad luck," Hogben said around a yawn, "that we

half-broke the jam immediately. When they sent for us—we're
Sir Andrew's special pets, apparently, though I think he must
hate us more than he likes us because we get all the lousiest assignments ... Where was I? Oh, yes. They were getting blank
screens and no onward transmission. We came charging in and
blithely said, 'No problem! It's just the cypher-synch gone out of
kilter—look!' Bingo, the screens lit up for us. Only they proceeded to show this ridiculous garble."

Absently he tapped a code into the remote again; the screens
replied with another selection of incomprehensible letters:
HJVGR WROPA MCRKE ...

"Which," Dilys Prinkett sighed, "at once convinced them we
could work the rest of the trick. Even when we'd discovered that
we couldn't, they took until now to believe we needed help.
Well, at least you finally showed up. Can we kip down, please?
I'm *so* tired ..."

Barring a short break to eat a hasty meal, which failed to live
up to Sir Andrew's assurances about edibility, the team ham-
mered away at the job until past one in the morning. They
ruled out one fault after another, confirming as they did so two
of Acey-Acey's most cherished advertising claims: that their
gear was exceptionally reliable, and that fault-tracing on the X
Ten Thousand was exceptionally easy.

But even when, using a phone in one corner of the room, they
called for and were brought a substitute portable read-in—just
in case the flaw lay there rather than in the main part of the machinery—they found nothing wrong at all.

"It has to be in the programming," they agreed at last, and
dismally sat down to tabulate the likeliest ways in which a log-
jam could have arisen. Every attempt to come up with an alternative possibility proved fruitless; they returned time and again
to the one Desmond had originally defined—an unpredictable
clash between at least two and conceivably several instructions
which the machines interpreted as referring to contradictory or
even perhaps nonexistent programmes.

All the time the TV cameras wove back and forth, spying on them.

"I'm exhausted," Molesey finally announced. "And so are the rest of you, right?" He stretched as he rose from his chair. "I recommend we sleep on it and see if we have any new ideas in the morning."

"Ah . . ." Desmond intervened. "There are only four bunks in the room next door, you know."

Molesey started. "No, I didn't know! What do the idiots expect us to do—use the floor?"

As though answering a cue, Dilys Prinkett came in, yawning, her clothes crumpled, not looking particularly refreshed by her rest.

"Say, you lot must be beat by now," she said. "Bill is still snoring his head off, but if you want to take over the bunk I was using, one of you . . . Any progress?"

"None at all."

"Think there's anything that can be done?"

"Not until we have something to match the encrypted material with."

"Good, that makes us a unanimous majority. Dr Molesey, I overheard Sir Andrew saying to that awful Finbow woman that he's left numbers where he can always be reached at the switchboard here. Suppose you call him up and say we want to go home?"

"I'll do that!" Molesey said, and headed for the phone. After a couple of minutes' fruitless argument he slammed it back on its hook.

"He left numbers where he can be reached, okay! But he also left orders that he mustn't be disturbed unless we fix the trouble!"

"I'll be damned!" Crabtree said, speaking for them all. A moment elapsed in silence full of suppressed fury.

"Look—uh . . ." Desmond spoke up. "I'm not feeling sleepy yet. And Dilys has had at least some rest. Why don't you three use the bunks that are vacant? I'll take over Bill's when he wakes up."

"Well, if you're sure—?" Molesey said, brightening.

"Yes, go ahead; I'm quite okay."

Desmond was no longer okay an hour later. For a while he and Dilys talked desultorily, mostly about working for the Post Office Telecommunications Centre, which had been one of the options open to him when he left university. He asked what conditions were like in the Civil Service.

"Frankly," she answered with a scowl, "I think you made the right choice. I don't know which makes it worse, the fact that the whole setup is paranoid or that the people in charge are as hidebound as a family bible!"

"Uh . . ." He pointed discreetly at the nearer of the TV cameras.

"What are you on about—? Oh, those things! Don't worry. They're very unlikely to play over the tape."

"Tape?"

"Sure, those monitors are on automatic overnight. They aren't primarily intended as a bugging system, at least not in the conventional sense. The people who designed this place were worried in case some super-subtle brain-bending gas might find its way through the air-conditioners, so they rigged these cameras everywhere to make sure medical personnel could spot the very first signs of aberrant behaviour among the *lucky* survivors. Christ, it's a lunatic world we live in anyway, isn't it? And after the big smash it would be even crazier, so I honestly don't know how they hope to tell the normal from the abnormal. When you meet some of the power-hungry maniacs I've run across . . ."

The words dissolved into a yawn. "Sorry, I'm a lot less rested than I thought I was."

"You sound very embittered," Desmond ventured.

"Should I not be? Megalomania is kind of an occupational

disease among politicians, and sometimes I suspect they suffer from even worse afflictions."

She yawned again, immensely wide, and her eyelids drifted shut and she twisted around on her chair and in another few moments was fast asleep.

Left to his own devices, Desmond slipped off his shoes because his feet were getting sore, and set to pacing restlessly back and forth around the room. He knew it would be wise to try and sleep even if he had to make do with some cushions and a patch of floor. But something was preventing him. Something was hovering at the edge of his mind like the ghost of an itch. At last he stopped in his tracks, folded his fingers into fists, and compelled himself to concentrate.

At first it was like trying to trap the images of a dream. But by dint of pure determination he finally nailed down the crucial clue.

Oh, surely they can't have overlooked that possibility? Or—or could they? It didn't come up during our discussion!

He had managed to recapture a down-column news item, not from a professional journal but from an ordinary paper, which he had noticed ... how long ago? A year, two years? Never mind! The point was this. An American bank had run into precisely this sort of trouble; a tiny oversight had rendered their computer facilities unusable. That case too had involved a cypher. How exactly had it happened?

Shutting his eyes, he forced half-forgotten details back to awareness. This bank—*that's it!*—protected its customers' financial records by encrypting them in a manner similar to but less elaborate than the one in use here. And the cypher was changed at intervals of about one hundred days. And the time came when on a date that seemed entirely random the computers refused to part with any of their stored data.

After hours of fruitless struggle the engineers quit for the night, and when they returned everything functioned perfectly.

Then, and only then, they figured out what had gone wrong. The machines had been instructed to discontinue the outgoing cypher as of Day 200, and start with the replacement on Day 201 . . .

"I wonder!" Desmond said softly to the air.

Plainly it was no use telling these machines that the date was today, or yesterday, or tomorrow. But suppose one were to detour completely around the date-component?

Shaking, because he could scarcely believe so simple a solution might work—indeed, feeling rather foolish under the unwinking gaze of the TV cameras, because if the people in charge here did ever replay any of their videotapes tonight's surely would be the one they'd pick—he walked over to the trolley bearing the remote read-in and carefully tapped into its keyboard a date which certainly would not have any random alphabets assigned to it because it was the day on which he had been born. And he appended the first command that came to mind.

28 April 1950. Print contents of Store G.

There was a brief pause. Then, with stolid mechanical regularity, words in comprehensible English began to march across the display screens.

At first he was dumbfounded at his unexpected success. Then he felt a surge of triumph and delight, and for want of anyone else to share it with turned with the intention of waking Dilys.

And *then* he caught sight of what the nearest screen was showing.

Following a code reference, it ran:

CAPE TOWN. *Obtain soonest intact copy Boersma Report on retardation of intelligence among Bantu by denying protein foods in infancy. Intention here withdraw free milk from schools. Essential determine probable efficacy and/or need for more drastic action.*

That couldn't possibly mean what it appeared to mean! Could it . . . ?

He stood rock-still, mouth dry, the sound of his bloodstream deafening in his ears. And remembered. Yes, only a few years ago the government had indeed cancelled the long-standing free issue of milk to schoolchildren.

Abruptly he was gazing wildly from one screen to another. Perhaps because the circuitry was confused by having to print out on a date before it came into existence, all four screens were displaying different texts, and they were coming and going with dizzying rapidity. Had he not been since childhood an extremely fast reader he would not have taken in more than an occasional ambiguous phrase; as it was, among many other items which were totally meaningless to him he managed to catch message after whole message whose implications were unspeakably terrifying. Immobile but for his eyes, he endured their impact.

WASHINGTON. *Regret unfeasible discontinue Open University owing widespread popular enthusiasm. However will ensure safe content all course materials especially history/political science/economics. Intention displace radical staff and render funding subadequate owing inflation. Disillusionment expected soonest.*

DUBLIN. *Imperative prevent rapprochement Dublin/Stormont. Essential troops receive blooding under conditions nearidentical mainland cities. Query useful furnish arms/explosives IRA Provisionals. Request recommend suitable neutral intermediary.*

ATHENS. *Apologise government derogatory references BBC World Service. Assure FM regularisation both world and internal broadcasting well in hand. Situation numerous disaffected personnel already rendered intolerable. Resignations expected momently. Replacements in view significantly more tractable.*

BRUSSELS. *Predict doubling/trebling UK property prices within year. Building concentrated commercial/luxury sector. Lowcost housebuilding seen near standstill soonest. Mortgages shortest supply. Little/no competition foreign purchasers. Excellent return assured. Regret unfeasible demolish 1500 homes for London Ringway as intended. Otherwise few setbacks to fulfillment of forecast.*

BONN. *Expect on schedule quota skilled/semiskilled labour promised as condition entry EEC. Housing shortage usefully contributes desire emigrate. Three day week scheduled end 1973 certain create adequate unemployment. Confrontations to include miners railwaymen other unpopular minority unions. Hope for riots/disorders requiring committal of troops from Ulster. Recommend commence withdrawal workpermits Turks/Greeks/Yugoslavs as arranged.*

By now he was shaking so violently, he had to cling to the steel trolley at his side. His teeth were threatening to chatter, but that would have distracted his attention. He set his jaw grimly and went on reading.

BERN. *Flotation poundsterling foreseen equivalent devaluation 20% or better. Soonest move all approved private holdings into DM/SwFr/FrFr prior official announcement. Pay no attention preliminary denials.*

COPENHAGEN. *Obscenity legislation in draft capable of extension from basis fullscale censorship. Bound however prove controversial. Meantime assistance your end indispensable. LCJ complains profits reduced over half by unauthorised imports erotica. Threatens discontinue generous party contribution unless action immediate. Proceeds from resale customs seizures also seriously affected.*

TEHRAN. *Inform Shah £3,000,000,000 acceptable provided (a) large portion offset by armaments (b) commission to us increased from 1% to 1½%. Will send representatives St Moritz privately confirm details method of payment.*

THE HAGUE. *Miners demands now exceed £40,000,000. Policy of presenting claim to public as blackmail successful so far. However suggestion we compulsorily purchase all oilbearing ground UK useful means reduce their economic leverage. Convey thanks to parties responsible.*

Intellectually he was aware that the messages were being displayed no faster than before. It must just be an illusion due to the pattern that was emerging, a pattern which enabled him to put two and two together almost instantaneously, which was making him feel as though he were at the centre of an artillery bombardment.

ACCRA. *Growing discontent with Health Service detectable. Numerous coroners censure doctors/nurses poor knowledge English. Suggest further reduction linguistic qualifications medical personnel seeking admission UK view prospective snowball effect.*

SALISBURY. *Many radical community-relations personnel dismissed. Seeking means eliminate remainder. Damaging information re black Rhodesians resident UK requested soonest.*

HAMILTON BERMUDA. *Assure RVW no intention persecute property developers. Recent ministerial statements ignorable. However advise delay return UK postelection.*

TOKYO. *Heathrow exercise deemed unsatisfactoriest. Query possible divert proarab hijack Londonwards. Atrocities excessively remote UK public despite letterbombs etc.*

ANDORRA. *Continuance policy nonprosecute income tax avoidance warranted. Collectors instructed court proceedings applicable small sums only. Inform OBK.*

ALL BWI. *Extinction streetlights unreflected increased crime-rate here. Armed police still generally undemanded. Query applications to hand of known violent persons desiring admission UK.*

LISBON. *Worry re infection Portuguese workers radical notions needless. Dissident personnel Health Service/BBC/teaching/socialwork discouraged. Many resignations.*

ROME. *Position faithful secured. Additional to reductions schoolfood and slumclearance current restrictions government expenditure create bookshortage schools/universities. Protests re birthcontrol/abortion continue. Also surveillance/publicity women cohabiting view prevent obtaining national assistance. Advise HH.*

MADRID. *Number of troops with Ulster service exceeds forecast. Confidently predict mass popular support their deployment against unions/immigrants/media/students/teenage gangs. Establishment disciplined efficient corporate state foreseen prior 1980.*

All of a sudden it was too much. He slammed shut his eyes to escape any more of the messages and had to—*had* to—scream at the top of his lungs.

Distantly he heard Dilys Prinkett asking what was the matter, and the rest of the trouble-shooting team came rushing in to put the same question.

Forcing his eyes open again, finding that by now the display on the screens was over because Store G had printed out everything it contained, he told them. As best he could. He kept stumbling over his tongue.

When he had finished they exchanged sad glances and attempted to verify his assertions.

Bewildered, Desmond realised that they could not. The log-jam could only be broken once. And still nobody knew how it had come about.

When he started to rant and howl with frustration they ran to the phone and called for help.

"By the way," Sir Andrew inquired of Dr Molesey after conveying fulsome thanks—by phone—to him and the other members of the trouble-shooting team, "is there any improvement in the condition of poor young what's-his-name?"

"Desmond Williams? No, I'm afraid not. I called the hospital this morning, and the psychiatrist in charge of his ward said he'd never run across such stubborn and detailed delusions of persecution. But he held out some hope; it's possible the condition may yield to electroshock treatment."

"What a shame, what a dreadful waste!" Sir Andrew sighed heavily. "Having had such a brilliant insight and solved our problem for us in next to no time ... Still, they do say, don't they, that genius is to madness next akin? I doubt if he'll appreciate it, but if you happen to see him perhaps you'd pass on a message from my Minister. He told me yesterday that not only he himself but the entire Cabinet including the PM are very much obliged by what young Williams did."

The Suicide of Man

This is a story with a happy ending. The beginning, on the other hand . . .

Well, after all his care, all his precautions, there was absolutely no way he could not be dead.

And yet he wasn't. There were presence, consciousness, alarm, associated emotions. That which had been "I" for him was undestroyed.

He contrived an utterance, half a scream and half a desperate question. They answered, somehow.

What they told him was: "You are a ghost."

*I*t was a place, no doubt about that. In fact it was a recognisable room, with a solid floor and solid walls and a solid ceiling that shed gentle light and even a piece of furniture which supported him in a relaxed posture. Also he was not alone. There were three with him, of whom one was definitely a man and two were indisputably women. But he was more concerned about himself. He looked down and discovered his familiar naked skin with scars from, at last count, eight unsuccessful operations. He identified the hands he had once been so proud of because they were deft and subtle. He knew his own limbs, his very body-hairs . . .

And was dazed and horrified and ultimately appalled.

Someone said, and he believed it was the woman who stood nearer of the two, "In your vocabulary we find no better referent for a person who is neither alive nor dead. You were Lodovico Zaras. You were a professor of experimental psychology. You fell victim to a form of cancer which disseminated rapidly. You decided in a year which you called by the figures one-nine-seven-eight that you would rather cease than continue to endure operations which could at best postpone your death but never cure the sickness. Is this what you recall?"

He replied, not quite understanding how he was able to speak at all, let alone do so in response to statements he knew not to be in English or Spanish or French or any other tongue he was acquainted with, "Yes, but how can I remember anything? I killed myself!"

Again the flat assertion: "You are a ghost."

At the moment of his death he had been sitting in a favourite chair, with the glass from which he had drunk his remedy for existence on a table at his side, a favourite recording of Bach's organ music ringing in his ears.

He was sitting (again?) now, on what was not except by remote derivation a commonplace chair. He could and did stand up, feeling no twinge of pain, none of that old stubborn heaviness in the limbs which cancer had weighed down. He felt ethereally light. Yet he did not perceive himself as immaterial; when he clapped his palms together there was a noise and the contact stung, and stare how he might he could not see through his hands.

"Ghost?" he repeated in bewilderment.

From somewhere the man who was in the room produced an object he could name although its form was strange. It consisted of a reflector surrounded by a frame; it was a mirror.

"Look for yourself," the man invited, and he did, and he failed to find what he was looking for. What he saw was the mirror.

Empty of his image.

Because of that he grew extremely frightened, but there was something worse to follow.

"Touch me," said the woman who had spoken before, and came to stand in front of him. For a long moment he hesitated, so disturbed by not seeing his reflection that he needed to register every sense-datum he could. The ceiling was white and luminous. The walls wore the rich, profound blue of a distant horizon. The floor was green and reminded him of spring grass. This before him was, yes, was a woman: taller than himself, slender, with an avian fineness of bone, not beautiful but so un-

usual—indeed so improbable—that if he had hurried along a
street where she was walking the other way he would have
checked and looked back, astonished at her having not enough
black hair beginning too high on her forehead, ceasing too high
on her nape, amazed at those over-long legs which endowed a
child-size torso with the height of an adult, disturbed above all
by the implication that while being very surely human she was
also something . . . other.

Moreover she was naked, as he was.

Or was she?

There was something . . .

But it hurt his eyes, and he had to blink, and as his lids came
down she repeated her command in a more urgent manner,
holding up her thin right hand.

Diffident, he complied when the blink was over, and felt
warm convincing flesh, perhaps a little sparse over the bones.

"I can touch you and I cannot see my own reflection," he said
after a while. Giddying, the clash between the apparent reality
of this alien woman and the plain incontestable nonreality of
himself who could not make a mirror give back his portrait
made him tremble and sway.

"But if I touch you . . ." the woman said, and reached out,
and with a quick sidelong gesture like an axe-blow demonstrated how she could pass her own hand through his. Or—no!
Where his hand seemed to be. He felt nothing, except the phantom of a chill, yet he witnessed and would have sworn on his life
to the reality of her action.

Gasping, and realising in the same moment that he could de-
tect no rush of air into his lungs, he cried out, "I don't understand!" Still not knowing, either, how he could talk.

The man advanced, his face—which was too long, too
skimpy, too much dominated by vast eyes—set in an expression
of concern and regret.

"Lodovico Zaras, before we proceed with explanations, we
must offer our deepest and most sincere apologies. It is to be
hoped that a person such as yourself, a pioneer in your own day,

an intellectual explorer as it were, may forgive the presumptuous interference we plead guilty to. I speak to you as what you were, not what you are, but I trust that the difference has not yet become unendurable. Inevitably the burden of that difference will grow greater as time passes, but we hope and predict that the series of shocks you are due for will be slow enough for you to make adjustments and ultimately grant us the forgiveness which we beg of you now. I am Horad. It is not a name as you would understand a name, but more of a title, which I think you would find meaningless. My companions, of whom the same ought to be said, can be addressed as Genua"—who had passed her hand through his—"and Orlalee."

Still in the grip of that impulse which had dictated his suicide, he nonetheless failed to prevent his mind from setting to work on the data offered. It had been his curse since childhood that he could not bear mental inactivity. The prospect of having to lie like a dummy for yet another year in a hospital bed, when he had hoped the latest operation might also be the last, had been what drove him to knock on the doors of death. There were drugs aplenty to cure pain; those which cured boredom were not recognised as part of the pharmacopoeia, and most were illegal.

He said at length to Horad, "If I try and touch you . . ."

"Do so!" Horad held up his right arm. It felt much like Genua's, slim to the point of being scrawny. But . . .

There was something about these three which had already prevented him from thinking of them as merely naked, though none of them wore what he was accustomed to regarding as a garment.

In the case of Horad, it was far more striking than it was on Genua. It registered on his eyes as a zone where it was hard to focus; on his skin, as a vibration or a tingling; most, though, it impinged directly on his mind as a—a—

A state as much between *something* and *nothing* as he himself was between *alive* and *dead*.

On the women it might have passed for some form of protective garb; after all, who can predict what will happen in the vicinity of ghosts? But on Horad it could be—could be *detected* all around his head, across his shoulders, down his upper arms . . . To look at him any other way except straight in those excessive eyes was to be gravely disturbed by . . . *it.*

Lodovico swallowed: nothing, not even his own saliva. Yet it was as though he did. He remembered what he had formerly experienced as the act of swallowing, and this was much like it, and had his attention not been on the act it might have passed as well as the real thing.

Faintly he said, "What have you made of me, that you think I ought to call myself a ghost?"

The three exchanged pleased looks. Orlalee spoke up for the first time.

"We hope to be able to answer that question first of all. We need, however, to know how you perceive us before we can choose the proper terms to express our intended meaning. How do we seem to you?" And they struck poses for inspection.

He looked them over in detail as best he could, still finding it impossible to study certain areas of—no, that was inexact: *around*—Horad. He found all three alike in their fragility and near-hairlessness; on their respective pubes there was only down, not actual hair. Their feet, as he looked lower, he found to be high-arched, with the toes reduced to simple stubs, the nails to thin pale lines.

He pondered the implications, disregarding one sick notion which had briefly occured to him: that he might be in Hell. There was no torment in his mind at the moment other than the sense of need-to-know-unsatisfied which had always been an integral part of his personality. On the contrary! He was in a dream-like state of elation all of a sudden. In his mind, such total terror that it made him want to dissolve into eternal darkness balanced and teetered back and forth in competition with a sense of excitement he had not enjoyed since he was a boy, the excitement due to comprehending in the guts those abstract concepts which he knew his teachers were merely mouthing. He fancied for a moment he might do to these people what he had loved to do to his instructors, and surprise them. And abandoned the idea at once. On the other hand, conceivably he might please them.

Licking (or that was what it felt like) his lips (or what in this version of "I" now felt like lips), he said (or used whatever communication channel had been allotted him), "I think you must be people, but so much later than me that I don't suppose you can tell me what the date is."

For a very short time he was alone. The period elapsed was so brief by his standards, he might have dismissed it as an illusion but that on returning Horad said, "Excuse us, please. We were delighted by your response and wished to be-personal in conveying news of it."

The hyphenation of "be-personal" was audible (?) to Lodovico; this was a clearly identifiable proof that the language he was speaking (?) was none of his own time.

And in the same thought came awareness of the truth that he must no longer say "own"; he could, however, say "former."

Orlalee said, "We were particularly pleased that you have been able to express a significant truth. We are people, in part of the sense you would use the term. We are also much evolved past where you were. And if we were to try and give you a date, it might well be wrong by several thousand years."

"Revolutions of the planet," said Genua, "are not as important now as they were for you."

Lodovico experienced a biting-lower-lip sensation. He felt real to himself; these people were talking to him as though he were real; yet when they tried to touch him they could not do what he could, locate solid substance.

It was not simple, but it was also not impossible to resolve the conundrum.

"You must have a means," he said slowly, "of projecting an effigy, a counterpart, a simulacrum, of a personality for which you stumbled on sufficient data to make it seem real to *itself*, and yet which you can only half-perceive. Perhaps you are having to force yourselves to believe in me, while I have no trouble accepting that I am here and now although I wished never to exist again."

He clenched his fists.

"But being what you have made me, what am I—what can I do or be? Any world but mine must be illusion to me!"

"We could not ask permission in advance," said Orlalee, who was both fairer-haired and darker-skinned than Genua. It was impossible to determine whether she was either in respect of Horad owing to the vagueness he sort-of-wore. "This was because until we did it there was nothing of which permission might be obtained. Now there is. We will accordingly accept your instruction if you say: *desist!*"

They waited.

Eventually he said, looking past them at the blank blue walls, "First tell me what I can and cannot do. Do I—do I eat? Drink? Sleep, suffer, become intoxicated?"

Still they waited, until he forced out the last part of the multiplex question.

"I feel weak, only half-real. Have you resurrected me so that I must face death a second time?"

"You are a collective percept," Horad said. "As yet you are not strong because only we three perceive you. We hear you speak; it is not with sound. We see where you are, but it is not with light. We and you interact, but if we did not agree to perceive you there would be nothing."

"Yet I perceive myself!" Lodovico burst out. "I am aware!"

"That is because without your perception of yourself there would be nothing for us to perceive. We did not choose that this be so; it turned out to be of the nature of the universe."

He wrestled with that for a while and eventually gave a feeble shake of the head.

"We may have some difficulty here," Orlalee said. "We are uncertain of the parameters you ascribed to a definition of 'consciousness' in your age. We have faint echoes of certain theories, but no indication of which if any you subscribed to. Permit us to question you on this subject and by stages our explanations will become more lucid."

"Ask away," Lodovico invited, folding his arms on his chest.

"When you killed yourself," Genua said, taking a step closer to him, "did you expect to re-awaken in a paradise or a place of torment?"

"I didn't expect to wake at all," was his prompt and emphatic answer. "Since boyhood I've been resigned to the fact that consciousness was a by-product of material existence. The fact that I seem to myself to be here, now, whenever and wherever the here-and-now may be, indicates that I must have been nearly right. You just told me that if I did not perceive myself you would have nothing to perceive, and moreover that I am a weak percept because no one apart from you three perceives me—Wait, I should re-phrase that. No one else *is perceiving* me."

"Could that"—from Horad—"have been expressed in the language of your time?"

"Yes!" the answer snapped back. "When I said it I wasn't aware of using a language I didn't grow up with."

Three smiles.

"Oh, we have chosen very well," Orlalee said. "Faced with the logical contradiction of being aware when he is-and-knows-he-must-be dead, he makes statements concerning not the self which cannot be present but the self which he's currently observing by being it. I judge that you, Lodovico, while surprised and startled at being imitated, are not angry."

"Angry?" He pondered, or imagined or suspected or believed or [a thousand possibilities] that he did. Eventually he said, "No, I don't think I have enough strength in the version of me which you three are perceiving to become angry. But in any case I would hope not to be. I would prefer to be fascinated by a unique chance, if it is unique, and even if it isn't I'd like to add something unforeseen and almost unimaginable to the total of my experience. It must be very long after my own epoch.

"But you have survived. In my time, for a while at least, we were afraid mankind might not. It follows that you must have cured the problems which worried us. I find I'm fascinated by the idea of seeing a far-distant future civilisation, even though I may find many aspects of it incomprehensible. If I seem dull-witted, bear with me. Evolution must have taken place on the mental as well as the physical plane."

"Yes, that is true," Horad confirmed. "Still, the fact that we have been able to establish communication argues that there is continuity between humans of your age and of this. I have thought of a way of expressing how much time has elapsed since your original existence. We are approximately as distant from you as you were from the creatures who spoke in grunts, shaped animal-horns and branches into tools, but were still terrified of fire and ate their food uncooked. Yet there are few differences in form between you and me: somewhat less hair—for instance I judge you were capable of growing a beard although you did not do so, whereas I am not—and longer limbs and smaller torsos and marginally greater cranial capacity. We mature later, sexually speaking; we have lost the ability to metabolise certain essential compounds from their chemical precursors, or in other words we require two more vitamins than you did. And there are other petty differences. Nonetheless we are equipped to communicate with you, while you could not have conversed with your correspondingly remote ancestor."

"Because I'm not myself even though I imagine that I am. In fact I'm only your collective percept." The statement was hurtful to utter, but Lodovico felt obliged.

"True. Remember, though, you are as exact a percept as we, with millennia of knowledge and skill you're unaware of, have been able to contrive," said Genua. "In your day, if what data have endured may be relied on, reconstructions of extinct primitive organisms had been attempted by combining fossil relics with guidelines based on species still surviving that had changed little over aeons. Not much later, some of the great reptiles were actually bred again from modified cousins or descendants. You

are the result of a corresponding technique applied to consciousness instead of physical shape."

"Why me?" Lodovico demanded.

"Chance brought us sufficient data to derive you. I regret to
say"—this from Orlalee with a wry smile—"it is not because
you became famous through the millennia!"

"No, I meant: why do it at all? Am I the first, or is this something you nowadays do routinely?"

"You are the very first," Horad said. "As for the underlying
reason . . ." He shrugged; it was curious to see how the gesture
had endured, and disturbing to see how differently the muscles
moved on that bird-light body . . . and most disturbing of all *not*
to see, because he couldn't bear to look, the matching move-
ment of the whatever-it-wasn't that Horad "wore."

"So I am an experiment," said Lodovico.

"That is so."

"You plan to study me? Interrogate me?"

"Naturally."

"And"—with boldness that surprised him—"is there any
bargain between us?"

"Yes, of course," Orlalee said. "Even before we commence
studying you, we wish you to agree that the trouble you are
being put to is justified. First, therefore, we must show you our
world. If, after inspecting it, you decide you would prefer not to
assist us, you may cease. Obviously we shall make another attempt, but we shall be resigned to the same outcome—and so on
and on, if necessary for many generations."

"It is unbefitting," said Genua, "to run counter to another's
will."

"All by itself that promise makes me like your world," said
Lodovico. "Show it to me."

Struck by a sudden thought, he added, "By the way . . . is it
still Earth?"

Visions of other solar systems blazed and faded in his mind in
a fraction of a heartbeat.

"Yes," Horad said. "After all this time, it is still Earth."

* * *

But an Earth its inhabitants had learned to love, with all its ulcers healed. It still had mountains and oceans and rivers, valleys and forests and plains, blue sky and white clouds that sometimes darkened and uttered the ancient bark of thunder. Almost at once, however, he began to notice changes. There were trees he could not put a name to. Friendly fish of no species he recognised came ambling up beaches on stubby leg-*cum*-fin limbs, and often as he was passing a flowered vine it would reach out in his direction and breathe a gust of perfume over him, then fall back quivering as though with unheard private laughter.

Essentially, though, the planet remained as recognisable as its people, and in all respects bar one the latter delighted him. He found the children charming, while young parents behaved to their offspring with such a natural, unpremeditated blend of firmness and tenderness that they might have been animals uncomplicated by theory and dogma.

This much was a fulfilment of his fondest dreams.

But the older folk! They frightened him! They were all sort-of-clad, and what they "wore" was the finished version of the thing (?) that made Horad hard to look at.

Certain of these old ones, Lodovico could not even turn his head towards.

"It is because in your former existence, although you possessed the sense by which you now perceive them, there was nothing for you to use that sense on." This by way of explanation from Orlalee. It left him more confused than ever, and she tried to amplify her statement.

"You think you are seeing them," she offered. "This is not so. You are detecting them by their act in perceiving you."

"You mean I am a percept to them, as well? To—to a bunch of *garments*?" He understood well, now, why a mirror could not reflect him; this, though, was a fresh cause for dismay.

"That is not clothing. It is self. It is an example of the principle which you already know about: the one which imposes that you be conscious of self before we can perceive you."

Lodovico struggled gallantly after that concept.

"You mean you could not have perceived me unless I'd been a conscious being instead of a dead corpse."

"A dead corpse can be made easily from common substances."

He gave up. Seeing his bafflement, Genua—who was also with him, as usual—attempted another route.

"We have made calculations," she said. "In your time, persons died commonly after fewer than a hundred revolutions around the sun. We live much longer. When age begins to erode our memories, we arrange to have ourselves remembered by what appears to you to be a garment. It is a version of one's own personality that permits growth to begin all over again. Progress from one self to another may continue for thousands of years, though of course the first and final personalities would not recognise each other."

"These—these 'other-selves' are independent entities, then?"

"No, they are wholly dependent. They are reflections, they are objectified echoes, never more than copies of the persons to whom they belong. You, on the other hand . . ."

Abruptly the implications of that curtailed sentence came storming in on Lodovico's mind. The world grew dark for an instant. When he could see clearly again, he found Horad was there too.

"Yes," said Horad in a grave and sympathetic tone. "That is what you are: the first such reflection of a self which belongs to someone who was born and lived his life in what to us is the far-distant past."

For a while after that revelation, there had to be an interruption in his exploration of this new age. But he made a good recovery and was able to go on.

There were no more cities. When he asked his companions how many human beings there were now they surprised and indeed alarmed him: they paused long enough to count . . . And could not quite agree on whether it was more or less than thirty million.

People lived far apart, yet did not actually live anywhere. They were forever on the move, deciding that the mood they happened to be in deserved that climate, that season, that landscape, and acting on the conclusion.

Certainly they had homes. He was entertained at several and admired them extravagantly, for they were beautiful in ways that combined the supreme architectural achievement of literally hundreds of civilisations. He could not even try to keep track of all the cultures, long-vanished now, from which he was being shown relics. Occasionally he thought he recognised something as Egyptian or Assyrian or Greek; when he inquired, he was given names he had never heard, Uglardic or Canthorian or Benkilese. . . .

Most agreeable of the survivals was the custom of celebrating by sharing food and drink, and beyond that scents and changes in the atmosphere which were sometimes more alarming than enjoyable, though all those around him seemed to know how to appreciate them. Feasts were held in his honour. He found he could taste, though he could draw no nourishment from, the miraculous dishes placed before him.

("You can eat, of course, since you are after your own fashion a person," Horad said. "But you need not. You are sustained by our awareness of you, and everyone you meet will make that existence stronger. We advise that you should eat if only because, perceiving that you do, we and everybody will find it easier to regard you as a real individual. If you enjoy the flavours, textures and scents, so much the better. We think of you as one who can." And he discovered the assumption was correct, though the logic behind it was still dream-like, tantalising, elusive.)

Art had lasted, but had spawned branches he could not see the purpose of. There was nothing for him in a communal ceremony which structured silence for a day and a night and a day, except boredom. Unable to become weary, he perforce witnessed the whole of it, and when the audience (?) roused and dispersed they were beaming with pleasure and showered compliments on the person who was part-host, part-administrator.

The going?

Belatedly he wondered about it, and realised that there was none. There was *being here*—interlude—*being there,* which automatically became *here* instead. He asked about it, and Genua said, "Again it is a talent which you possessed, but did not know of it because in your time there was nothing to provoke its operation. I cannot explain it; no one could. You must feel it as it is happening. Then in a little while you will go alone, without the help of me or Orlalee or Horad. If I were to say to you, 'Contract in succession the following muscles, which I point out on this chart, in each alternate leg, and then relax them in this precise order, and then to keep your balance do this and that with the muscles in your torso, arms and shoulders . . .' Well, how many steps would you take in a day? Be patient. Soon enough you will have the principle in your bones."

He was secure enough now to essay a joke. He said, "What bones?"

Also there was the counterpart of work. This above all was as he had dreamed it might be, shorn of repetitive drudgery, free from commercial pressures: a series of acts undertaken at places where people came together for purposes of production, knowing always why they did what they did and informed about the benefits they were giving to others. He spent days and days watching fascinated as even very small children conjured useful objects (or at any rate objects he was told were regarded as useful, though he did not understand their function) from plants, from banks of clay, from roiling streams foul with sulphurous stench and dung-brown silt. He was running out of names, even of concepts; what adults did they termed "working" was often as far beyond him as the other-selves he had mistaken for clothing.

Now the full force of his predicament hit him. He really was among people of a distant future age, and their thinking had changed even more than their bodily form. Hunting comparisons, he settled on the image of a convinced Christian from the Middle Ages set down in a twentieth-century community where nobody was bothered by the notion of living on a moving ball of rock instead at the fixed centre of the universe, where it was not considered in the least blasphemous to tamper with natural forms but on the contrary it was regarded as sensible and useful to modify and improve wild plants and even animals, to revise what that medieval person would think of as the handiwork of the Almighty, sacrosanct. He was pleased to have reached that image, for it offered a useful peg on which to hang the more unpleasant of his frustrations. There were many. Each passing day (not that he or anyone else to his knowledge was counting them) added to his sense of impotence and isolation.

At first he had been delighted by the sheer novelty of his experience. Then by stages he had grown angry at not being able to grasp everything he was shown. Occasionally he had been shocked, especially when he learned that eroticism had endured and was now integrated into several art-forms, to the point where there were adults whose equivalent of a career consisted in instructing children, from babyhood up, about the amatory potential of their bodies.

He knew *a priori* that this was another medieval-visitor reaction, but it cost him much effort to reframe his thinking. He had been intellectually aware that even in his own age love-making had largely been separated from procreation, and it was logical enough that in the long run the division should become effectively total.

But there were private reasons why he had never partaken of whatever benefits this situation entailed. After leading a bachelor's life during his twenties and saying he was wedded to his work, he had been just about to marry when he was informed about his cancer. After which, of course, he had abandoned hope of any permanent involvement—wife, family . . . Too little time was left.

* * *

"Did you have regrets?" asked Orlalee.

They were on a hilltop overlooking a plain dotted with brilliant flowers, beyond which a stormcloud loomed blue as newtempered steel. He could not remember how they came here.

He said, "Yes, I should have liked to bring up a child—one at least. But in another way, no. I made good use of what time I did have. I enjoyed myself, especially when I was finding out something new. In one respect I was unusually lucky. Ideas often came to me in dreams, and while most people's dreamimages turn out by light of day to be ridiculous, now and then mine proved to be sound, even important. Do you people still dream?"

"Of course."

"Why 'of course'?"

"It is in the nature of mankind to perceive unrealities as well as realities. You are a dream as much as you are a ghost, Lodovico. You are the fulfilment, the concretisation, of one of the oldest dreams humanity has ever had."

"That being—?"

"The dream of the dead. The return of those who are no more. Those cut off before due time. Is it not there that one should seek the germ of the concept 'ghost'?"

"That makes sense," he conceded after a moment's thought.

And then, unexpectedly, she asked, "Lodovico, how do you like being a ghost?"

Without realising how honest and unpremeditated his answer was going to be, he heard himself say, "Very well!"

"If the same occurred to me I think I would miss much. I should like to hear your reasons in the hope they will be accessible to me."

"First tell me this. When you put on the—other-self, is it the end of something for you? The conclusion of a stage of life, for example?"

"Oh, yes." There was something of sadness in her look. "It is exactly at the end of growth when we don them. To be fullgrown is also to be dying; there is no boundary . . . Well?"

Lodovico pondered. At length he said, "Yes, I miss a lot, too.

But much of what I miss is not to be regretted, like having a physical body that cancer could corrupt."

"It does not do so any more," Orlalee said. "But you do have a physical body."

"What?" The shock was wrenching. "But—!"

"Look."

She caught his arm in her thin but strong fingers, and clamped tight. After a moment she released him. Pale marks showed on his skin that took a minute or more to fade.

"I—" Lodovico put his hand to his forehead, giddily. "I . . .!"

"Yes, that is the word: I!" She was smiling, and suddenly she was not alone because Horad and Genua had joined them.

Horad said, "Congratulations, Lodovico. You are a reality to us. All those people now alive who have not personally met you have at any rate heard about you. Since you are present in the total awareness of the species, you exist."

"But—!" Inchoate arguments flared in his mind, on such grounds as conservation of energy. How could the mere process of perceiving someone convert that someone from an impalpable phantom into a solid living being?

"Now I can do something I wanted to do before which wasn't possible," Orlalee said, and put her arms around him and kissed him in a manner which was indescribably ancient, all bar the taste of her, which was new.

After which all three made love to him and proved him real.

There was a moment when he felt it would be amusing to say, "I am become a perversion incarnate."

But none of them got the point.

"Lodovico," Genua said later, "you have now seen our world. Do you approve?"

"Of those things which I understand in it, yes. Every ideal of my time seems to have come to pass. Between any person and any other there is peace. There is no jealousy, nor greed, because there is enough to satisfy everyone. Nobody lacks the chance to attempt, if not accomplish, his or her ambitions."

"Ah, there's the trouble," Horad said. "There are so many ambitions we can see no way to fulfil."

Startled, Lodovico said, "So many? What can they be?"

"Long ago, even as long ago as your original time, men dreamed of visiting other worlds and eventually the stars. Even to have explored the local planets would have been a great consolation. But we are here on Earth, are we not?"

"I had been wondering," said Lodovico slowly. "There must have been attempts."

"Indeed there were. People have circled the Sun more closely than Mercury does; they have dipped into the atmosphere of Jupiter, probed the frigid wastes of Pluto. But ... Well, for every attempt there have been countless failures. Come with us."

They were at a crumbled mound surrounded by lapping waves.

"From here," Orlalee told him, "a decadent culture tried to launch a ship directly to the stars. The venture was insane. There was an explosion which sank half a continent."

They were at a creeper-covered clearing in the midst of a great forest of pines and birches, where a snow-capped mountain loured down on them.

"A long time ago," Genua said, "people here trapped a bit of sun-stuff in a magnetic holder. It was not strong enough. There was a vast fire which lasted less than an eyeblink, and that too ended."

They were in a desert where sand-scratched rags of metal whined in a constant wind.

"It is believed," murmured Horad, "that this is the only spot where men ever held converse with another intelligence. What was said, we shall never know. It was uttered in the form of radiation such as only a star can emit. Perhaps it was a star which answered us, focusing its signal on less space than my arms can span. That was recently. You see the desert; plants have not had time to claim it back."

The pattern grew in Lodovico's mind.

A person is fragile. Out where stars send messages to one another it takes a great deal to shield and protect a human body. Moreover the person who makes the voyage must spend so much time thinking about sheer survival, it is nearly a waste of time. So long goes by; so little is discovered!

"And what," he asked at last, "does this have to do with me?"

"Everything," they said. It was not Horad who spoke, or Genua, or Orlalee; it was the combination.

"Why?"

"You are immortal."

"Impossible!"

"Oh, no. On the contrary." This was definitely Horad. Lodovico had grown to recognise and like his manner: a trifle dry, often witty, always individual. "Perfectly possible. We intended it to happen, and it worked out."

"How, though? How?"

"Because of the way you have been created. You are a compound percept: we have explained this already. Now, even to us who were present when you first impinged on a present-time consciousness, you are solid. You must eat and drink, or you would die. You are in every respect bar one a person like any other."

"The difference," Orlalee said, "is that we cannot conceive of any means whereby you might be destroyed."

"But you just said I can die—" Lodovico began.

"By your choice. Your own choice. No other way," said Orlalee.

"Not the brutal gales of a gas-giant planet," Horad said soberly, "nor the furnace heart of a star can abolish what to us constitutes Lodovico Zaras. For you *are not* Lodovico Zaras. You are his incorruptible, indissoluble, inerasable image upon the consciousness of all mankind."

"We can imagine you choosing to starve yourself to death rather than perform the service we hope from you," said Genua. "But the necessity will not of course arise. Were that to be your decision, even now we could arrange that you cease to exist. But we could not do it against your will."

"Service?" Lodovico repeated.

"Before we tell you what it is," Horad said, "we must emphasise that there is a good reason why you should say no. Now that we have made you real, you can feel pain."

"I was used to that in my original self," Lodovico said slowly. "Why should it be different, this time?"

"Because we want you to go where no one else can go, and come back and tell us what it's like."

He thought that over for a while, and said at last, not looking at them, "And this will hurt."

"Yes. As nearly as we can calculate, you will be hurt more than any other human being who ever lived. Worst of all, you will never have an escape route into death."

It was not until a long time afterwards that he said yes.

They had been right about the pain. It was clear, it was a simple fact, that no human being had any right to stand by the bank of a river running liquid helium, on the side of Pluto currently turned away from the sun, and admire the way its flow competed with gravity. Yet . . . he did it.

Perhaps it was that for him pain no longer portended danger, inasmuch as he knew he would not die until humanity became extinct. The agony, at all events, was transformed, and little by little he became able to endure it.

It diminished, indeed, so rapidly, that even at the conclusion of his first expedition it paled into insignificance alongside the frustration he felt when he struggled to fulfil his part of the bargain. How to explain in words the sensation of cold so violent it was like a flame? How to describe the river's colour, which lacking hue and brilliance and saturation was nonetheless seared into his memory like a scar?

Paradoxically, those who had sent him forth were well pleased. He had imagined failure, rejection; instead, when they had healed him they showered him with compliments and asked how soon he would be ready to leave again. (His going was by the route he had been taught since his resurrection. Any of the people who questioned him about what he had discovered could have taken it too, but for them it was useless when the destination was empty space or the surface of a hostile planet. He alone, none other, could survive a visit to a place like that.)

Among those who came to congratulate and thank him, he nearly did not recognise Horad because his other-self was more striking now, more disturbing to the vision . . . even though Lodovico had grown to accept that its essence was his. Natural human flesh clearly could not take the punishment he had consented to endure. Therefore . . .

To Horad he put a question which went some short distance towards relief of his frustration; from Horad he received an answer which sustained him on the rest of his journey.

He said, "How is it that you people have drawn so much from the little I was able to convey in words?"

And Horad explained, "It is long past your epoch, Lodovico. For us, communication is not confined to speech. No more, to be candid, was it for you; for the most part, it seems, you imagined that it was, but in practice what you took for misunderstandings were very often the result of someone understanding another person 'only too well.' "

With a final dry coda: "That phrase has no equivalent in any modern language, because in this tongue we are speaking there is the facility to make quotation-marks."

All of which was a supreme achievement by an admirably evolved modern mind, a condensation into a few sentences of millennia-worth of reflection and analysis.

And because he understood this brief reply with such clarity even though it belonged to a much later age than his own, Lodovico was able to convince himself that the people of today were worth suffering for.

He went again. Again. Again.

They grew afraid. It had not been calculated that he should become obsessed with his travels to unsurvivable environments. Whenever they tried to tell him he had done enough, however, he ranted and raved until they let him depart one more time.

By stages they became resigned. They had created him. He was now himself. The creators had long ago lost control. It remained to derive what data they could from having him to talk to, or simply be with. Mad, wild, primitive, berserk?

Unique.

But offering—still miraculously offering—reports that others could study and transform into comprehensible, and thus into fascinating, information.

It had been a long time, as the psychic evolution of the human species went, since there was anything their ancestors might have termed *news* . . .

They therefore tolerated it that he should learn: yes, they grow in Jupiter and Neptune and Uranus! Variously, from viciously to vicariously! (What does it mean? It means itself because no human ever before perceived it!)

As it became less than a marvel to him, for after all it was merely a not-Earth event and belonged to this universe, to this galaxy, this planetary system (shrinking by orders of magnitude with each review), he was able to describe his experiences in plainer terms.

In Uranus a creature ate him, fifty thousand miles long, and he survived. This among a million other recollections.

Naturally.

Neptune was the place where a sort-of-a-volcano was erupting icy lava at a yard per year and the nearby flora evolved to meet the threat and, as he watched, learned how to run at twice that speed. Again, among countless less communicable data.

As for Jupiter: there *something* greeted him, and told such a monstrous lie, he came home persuaded it must be true on some other axis of perception. But he did not at once insist that he should go back, preferring to postpone a second meeting with—whatever.

Whereas Saturn . . . He treasured that especially, not only for the methane-bergs and ammonia-bows and geysers, not even for the rings, but because whatever they were they were delicious and so proud of it and flattered to know their taste was being appreciated for the first time by a being from elsewhere. They had never realised that elsewhere was. It shattered their consciousness like the shell around an exploding chick (but there were neither chicks nor shells for them because they were distinctly *other* and had he not been immortal tasting them—and being able to accept they were delicious—would have done much more than simply kill him) #because of which there were potentially several trillion qualifications to any statement he was able to bring back and obviously it was futile to struggle with the# NATHELEES they went looking for other consumers. It was a hurriness. By the end of his visit none were left but there was no need to regret the extinction of their species because they provided a symbol intimating #how he knew he didn't know but he #knew# and—and the hell with it # *gone to find the stars whatever they may be in the hope-identical-with-conviction they also eat us well.*

Nobody back on Earth liked that report. It was overshadowing. First time and they got it right, for a ridiculous purpose!

"But in what sense were they delicious?" demanded practical Orlalee, whom he had grown very much to iike.

"In the sense they couldn't help," returned Lodovico. "They had evolved toward that goal for a billion years."

"You being the collective percept of us all," Genua mused, "we imagined you would bring back information we could understand."

"Especially," Lodovico suggested with a *moue*, "because I belong to a less evolved age, and you comprehend my total consciousness."

"Perhaps," Horad said, "we'd have done better with a consciousness derived from our time."

"But you could not," Lodovico said. "You could not have recreated a personality as complex and modern as your own. I am at the lower limit of what you can derive from yourselves and externalise. Do not blame me, therefore, for my shortcomings; they are yours."

When they did not contest the statement, he added, "I am in luck. Being transported, as it were, to this time from another, far simpler age, I'm already primed with the assumption that there are many things I'm not equipped to grasp. Please stop thinking that because you could conjure me into existence you can do anything."

"Would it be fair to say"—this from Horad, in a pensive and leisurely tone—"that what consoles you for the horrors and agonies you go through is the impossibility of digesting even our tiny corner of the universe within one conventional lifetime?"

With emphasis Lodovico said, "No!"

"What, then?" All three of them seemed taken aback.

"In my old life I was resigned to the belief that, just as no observer can know both the speed and the position of a particle, so no consciousness can comprehend the universe which is the frame of its existence. That is among the facts which have not changed over the millennia.

"What I failed to appreciate was how much more important it is to *be-conscious* than it is to *comprehend*. Possession of even a meagre imagination permits the owner to envisage processes that are forbidden by the laws of nature. Therefore any consciousness automatically transcends its universe."

"You are sure of that in so short a time?" Horad breathed.

"I was led to believe," Lodovico said wryly, "that you were indifferent as to whether a time-span is long or short."

And he added, "May I now continue my explorations? Or do you have no further need of reports from me?"

"Indeed we do," said Orlalee. "We welcome them. They are and will remain unique."

"You mean you do not expect ever to go where I am going?"

Genua parried that question. She said, "Is there not a lot of the future still to come?"

The zone of the asteroids he found to be crowded with events, but almost all of them were of a similar kind: collisions. He had much time, while witnessing them; to ponder the implications of the conclusion he had voiced to Horad. It was no more than a matter of probability; however, given that this petty corner of the cosmos was typical of, if not the whole, then a very large volume of it, and given that he had met consciousness on several occasions already—what was more, versions of consciousness capable of recognising him as an aware being even before he identified them—such data convinced him that consciousness must be of the essence of the universe.

It changed his own view of himself-as-he-now-was. Instead of that lingering resentment he still fought against when he set out, he was overtaken by a sense of gratitude so intense it was almost happiness. It might have been on any other conformation of awareness that the chance to be-first fell. It fell to him. Therefore . . .

(After his long spell in the asteroid belt, they asked whether he had grown bored on his quest, and he replied, "Bored? It would be impossible. A man can who can grow old, fatigued, confused—he may feel boredom because it is senility in little. As you have made me, I am no longer vulnerable to it.")

The cratered plains of Mars—the wind-punished valleys of Venus—the bleak hot mask of Mercury . . . and at last, climactically, the Sun. He plunged from the corona to the core, and when he came back . . .

It took the longest time of all to heal him. Doing what he had done had strained the collective credulity of Earth, and he who had survived the crash of asteroids and the fall of methane avalanches was much less believed in than before.

And yet—and yet—it had been done ... *He* knew, who had also doubted the possibility. Gradually the means came clear to other people, and with conviction healing followed. The mechanism? It was not and never had been mechanism, but only that-which-does-the-perceiving, liberated.

So the time arrived when those whom he now called his friends were able to visit him and talk.

"You have suffered," said one or perhaps all three of them. "Do you regard it as worthwhile?"

"Yes."

"Why?"

"Because what has been wrong with humanity since the beginning is not wrong with me. We have always had the imagination that belongs with immortality, but we have been trapped in destructible substance. It is small wonder that in ancient times there were so many religions that insisted on a life after death. Even our dreams rebelled against the idea of dissolution."

"But it has been considered by many of the cultures we know about that death is a boon."

"Is it so regarded now?" Lodovico countered. "Now that you've achieved so many of our old ambitions—peace, plenty, freedom from fear?"

They exchanged glances. Or, more nearly: a glance was exchanged among the three of them.

"We doubt it," Horad said at last.

"And you are right." He uttered the words with fervour. "It is what it was first believed to be, a burden we have laboured under far too long. And how can you not credit this, you whose supreme achievement has been to create the other-selves, the reflections of your personae which make you halfway to immortal?"

"It is not that we disbelieve it," Horad said. And the other two seemed to join him in speaking. "It is that we did not until now realise how right we are. Before we evoked you, we had begun to wonder whether there might not be a proper time for a species to die, a time chosen by itself. Thanks to you, we have been satisfied on that score. We go to fix the date for the suicide of man."

He who had been crushed by clashing asteroids, who had been vaporised by the solar phoenix cycle and returned, was overwhelmed by the purport of that promise. When he recovered enough to formulate a counter-question, he found there was no listener to put it to. He was alone.

After he got over the need to rail and scream, very slowly the truth dawned on him.

His mode of thinking was ancient. Worse—it was primitive. At the heart of it lay an assumption he should have discarded long ago, only the idea had never previously occurred to him. It was by that assumption he had been misled.

He was used to taking for granted that he was *somebody.*

It was a measure of the success Horad and Genua and Orlalee had achieved that he should have gone on believing, or rather not worrying about, this aspect of his nature until now. He must, he realised, correspond in minute detail to the version of Lodovico Zaras who, aeons ago, had discovered that he was due to die of cancer and preferred to choose his own moment and his own way to leave the world.

But he *was-not* that person.

He-now was not some body. He was some one.

And the distinction was indescribably important.

Ghosts!

"You arrived at understanding," they said when they returned.

"Yes, slow on the uptake though I was."

"There will be others." The problem was dismissed with something like a casual wave. "For those who date back furthest, it is not improbable that centuries will go by while they gradually begin to perceive the universe as it is instead of in the manner which their gross, half-evolved brains allowed them to accept. But it is not of course the brain which matters, is it?"

Lodovico knew exactly what was meant. Now. And if he could do it, so could others. He said, "Have you chosen the date?"

"As nearly as we can. We have been at pains to calculate in the sort of terms you used to apply. In less than half a million years it will no longer matter what becomes of Earth. Let it freeze or burn, let it wander the interstellar gulf or fall into the heart of the sun. There will be no more men and women. We shall have recalled and re-perceived every human being who ever existed, free like you to go everywhere, experience everything, and survive to remember what happened. Thank you, Lodovico. You gave us precisely what we dreamed of. There can be no greater gift in time or space."

"But," he said, thinking of termination in his simple, primitive fashion, "if there are to be no more humans . . ."

"It is for the best reason," they replied. "We created you to help us determine whether our species has engendered as much consciousness as is proper to it. The fact that you are as-you-are is the evidence we wanted. The ambition of a rational, intelligent species is not as-much-as-possible, but *enough*."

"At Saturn I ran across a similar decision," Lodovico said. "I do not yet see what you mean. But in the certainty that I eventually shall, I am glad to abide by the conclusion of mankind."

"It is good," they said, and went about the necessary business.

So in ripe time it was done, and mankind died as a material species. But its hordes of ghosts were billions strong, and went to compare notes with strangers who had made the like discovery, to confirm or disprove what they had found out about the universe, and often enough learned they had been wrong.

Often enough to keep them curious and intrigued for at least the current cosmic cycle. Even immortality cannot shrink the gap between the galaxies.

Sic fiat.

The Taste of the Dish
and the Savour of the Day

The Baron's circumstances had altered since our only previous encounter a year ago. This I was prepared for. His conversation at that time had made it abundantly clear that he had, as the charmingly archaic phrase goes, "expectations."

I was by no means sure they would materialise ... Still, even though I half suspected him of being a confidence trickster, that hadn't stopped me from taking a considerable liking to him. After all, being a novelist makes me a professional liar myself, in a certain sense.

So, finding myself obliged to visit my publishers in Paris, I dropped a note to what turned out to be an address the Baron had left. He answered anyway, in somewhat flowery fashion, saying how extremely pleased he would be were I to dine with him *tête-à-tête* at home—home now being an apartment in an expensive block only a few minutes from what Parisians still impenitently call *l'Étoile*. I was as much delighted as surprised; for him to have moved to such a location implied that there had indeed been substance in his former claims.

Yet from the moment of my arrival I was haunted by a sense of incongruity.

I was admitted by a man-servant who ushered me into a *salon*, cleanly if plainly decorated, and furnished in a style neither fashionable nor *démodé*, but nonetheless entirely out of keeping, consisting mainly of the sort of chairs you see at a pavement café, with a couple of tables to match, and a pair of cane-and-wicker armchairs. The impression was of a collection put together in the thirties by a newly-married couple down on their luck, who had hoped to replace everything by stages and found they couldn't afford to after having children.

I was still surveying the room when the Baron himself entered, and his appearance added to my feeling of unease. He

greeted me with a restrained version of his old effusiveness; he
settled me solicitously in one of the armchairs—it creaked abominably!—and turned to pour me an *apéritif.* I took the chance
of observing him in detail. And noticed . . .

For example, that although it was clean and crisply pressed
and was of excellent quality, the suit he had on this evening was
one I remembered from a year ago—then trespassing on, now
drifting over, the verge of shabbiness. His shoes were to match:
brilliantly polished, yet discernibly wrinkled. In general, indeed,
so far as his appearance was concerned, whatever he could attend to for himself—as his manicure, his shave, the set of his
tie-knot—was without a flaw. But his haircut, it immediately
struck me, was scarcely the masterpiece of France's finest bar-
ber.

Nor was his manner of a piece with what I would have pre-
dicted. I recalled him as voluble, concerned to create a memorable impact; in place of that warmth which, affected or not, had
made him an agreeable companion, there was a stiltedness, a
sense of going through formally prescribed routines.

He gave the impression of being . . . How shall I define it?
Out of focus!

Furthermore, the *apéritif* he handed me was unworthy of his
old aspirations: nothing but a commonplace vermouth with a
chip off a tired lemon dropped into it as by afterthought. For
himself he took only a little Vichy water.

Astonished that someone who, whatever his other attributes,
was indisputably a *gourmet,* should thus deny himself, I was
about to inquire why he was so abstemious. Then it occurred to
me that he must have had bad news from his doctor. Or, on reflection (which took half a second), might wish me to believe so.
I was much more prepared now than I had been a year ago to
accept that he was a genuine hereditary baron. However, even if
one is a scion of a family that lost its worldly goods apart from a
miserly pittance in the Events of 1789, one can still be a con-
man. There is no incompatibility between those rôles any more
than there is between being an author and being a sucker. So I

forbore to comment, and was unable to decide whether or not a shadow of disappointment crossed his face.

By the time when I declined a second helping of that indifferent vermouth, I might well have been in the mood to regret my decision to re-contact the Baron, and have decided to limit my visit to the minimum consistent with politeness, but for an aroma which had gradually begun to permeate the air a few minutes after I sat down. It was inexpressibly delectable and savoury, setting my tastebuds to tingle *à l'avance*. Perhaps everything was going to be for the best after all. A dinner which broadcast such olfactory harbingers was bound to be worthwhile!

Except that when we actually went to table, it wasn't.

At my own place I found a sort of symbolic gesture in the direction of an *hors d'oeuvre*: a limp leaf of lettuce, a lump of cucumber, a soft tomato, and some grated carrot that had seen better days before it met the *mandoline,* over which a bit of salt and oil had been sprinkled. To accompany this mini-feast I was given a dose of dry white *ordinaire* from a bottle without a label. Before the Baron, though, the servant set no food, only pouring for him more Vichy water which he sipped at in a distracted manner while his eyes followed my glass on its way to my lips and the discovery that such a wine would have shamed a *relais routier sans panonceau.* His face was pitiable. He looked envious!

Of rabbit-food and immature vinegar?

I was so confused, I could not comment. I made what inroads I could on the plate before me, trying to preserve at least a polite expression on my own face. And thinking about the servant. Had I not seen the fellow elsewhere?

As he answered the door to me, I'd scarcely glanced at him. Now, when he came to check whether I'd finished with my first course—I yielded it with relief—I was able to take a longer though still covert look. And concluded: yes, I had seen him.

Moreover I recalled when and where. During my last trip to France, in Guex-sur-Saône where they had held that year's French National Science Fiction Congress—and incidentally where I had met the Baron—and what is more, he had been in the same car as the Baron.

But a year ago my host could not possibly have afforded a manservant! He had not even been able to afford his bill at the Restaurant du Tertre to which he had recommended, and accompanied, me and my wife and the friends we were with; he still owed me an embarrassing trifle of seven francs eighty which I was not proposing to mention again if he did not, because the meal had been—as he'd promised—incredibly good value.

The incongruities here began at last to form a pattern in my mind. Had he received the benefit of his "expectations" and then let silly pride tempt him into an extravagance he now regretted? Was it because, thinking a servant appropriate to his new station in life, he had hired one, that he still wore the same suit and couldn't afford to have his hair properly barbered? Was it economy rather than health that drove him to refrain from even such poor refreshment as a guest was offered in this apartment which, though in a smart *quartier,* either was furnished out of a flea market or hadn't been refurnished since what one buys at flea markets was last in style?

Hmm . . . !

The interior of the head of a professional writer is a little like a mirror maze and a little like a haunted house. From the most trivial impetus, the mind inside can find countless unpredictable directions in which to jump. While I was waiting for the main course to be brought in, mine took off towards the past and reviewed key details of our meeting in Guex.

Of all the science fiction events I have attended—and in the course of twenty-five years there have been not a few—that was the most chaotic it has been my misfortune to participate in. The organisers chose a date already preempted by a reunion of *anciens combattants de la Résistance,* so that all the hotels in the centre of town were full and we had been farmed out to somewhere miles away. It was, I suppose, entirely in keeping with the rest of the arrangements that on the last evening of the congress we should find ourselves, and the only other English people present—the guest of honour, his wife, and their baby—abandoned in front of the cinema where the congress was being held because the committee and anyone else who was *au fait* had piled into cars and gone into the country for dinner. So many people had turned up for the reunion of the Resistance, there wasn't a restaurant in walking distance with a vacant table.

Hungry and stranded, we made the acquaintance of the Baron: a youngish man—I'd have said thirty-two and prematurely world-weary—lean, with a certain old-fashioned elegance, and out of place. I'd exchanged a word or two with him earlier in the day, when he'd chanced on me standing about as usual waiting for one of the organisers to put in an appearance so I could find out what was happening, and asked me whether a member of the public might attend the movie then showing, since he had a few hours to kill. Seemingly he had enjoyed the picture, for he had stayed over or come back for another.

Emerging now, drawing on unseasonable gloves with an air of distraction as though he were vaguely put out by the absence of a coachman to convey him to his next destination, he spotted and remembered me, and approached with a flourish of his hat to thank me for the trivial service I'd performed.

My answer was doubtless a curt one. Sensing something amiss, he inquired whether he might in turn be of assistance. We explained . . . choosing, of course, terms less than libellous, though we were inclined to use strong language.

Ah! Well, if we would accept a suggestion from someone who was almost as much a stranger as ourselves . . . ? (We would.) And did we have transportation? (We did, although my car was at the hotel twenty minutes' walk away.) In that case, we might be interested to know that he had been informed of a certain restaurant, not widely advertised, in a village a few kilometres distant, and had wondered whether during his brief stay in Guex he might sample its cuisine. He had precise directions for finding it. It was reputed to offer outstanding value. Were we . . . ?

We were. And somehow managed to cram into my car and not die of suffocation on the way; it's theoretically designed for four, but no more than three can be comfortable. Still, we got there.

The evening proved to be an education—on two distinct levels.

I found myself instantly compelled to admire the deftness with which our chance acquaintance inserted data about himself into a discussion about an entirely different subject. Even before I came back with the car the others had learned about his aristocratic background; I noticed he was already being addressed as *Monsieur le Baron*. His technique was superb! Always on the *qui-vive* for new tricks that might enable me to condense the detail a reader needs to know into a form which doesn't slow down the story, I paid fascinated attention. Almost without our noticing that he was monopolising the conversation, we were told about his lineage, his ancestors' sufferings at the rude hands of the mob, the death of the elderly aunt for whose funeral he had come to Guex, a lady of remarkable age whose existence he had been ignorant of until a lawyer wrote and advised him he might benefit under her will ... (The French are far less coy about discussing bequests than are we Anglophones.)

But on the other and much more impressive hand, within—I swear—five minutes of our being seated in the restaurant, the word had got around behind the scenes that someone of *grand standing* was present tonight. In turn the waiter—it was too small a restaurant to boast a head waiter—and the *sommelier* and the *chef* and finally the proprietor put in their successive appearances at our table as *M. le Baron* proceeded with the composition of our meal. He laid down that there should not be an excess of fennel with the trout, and that the Vouvray should be cellar-cool and served in chilled glasses but on no account iced, which would incarcerate its "nose" and prevent it from competing with the fennel (he was right); that with the subsequent *escalope de veau Marengo* one should not drink the Sancerre of which the *patron* was so proud but a Saint-Pourçain only two years old (he was right about that too), just so long as the *saucier* did not add more than a splash—what he actually said was *une goutte goutteuse*, a phrase that stuck in my mind because it literally means "a drop with the gout"—of wine vinegar to the salad dressing. And so on.

I was not the only one to be impressed. When we had finished our dessert, the owner sent us a complimentary glass apiece of a local liqueur scented with violets, wild strawberries, and something called *reine des bois* which I later discovered to be woodruff. It was so delicious, we asked where else it could be got, and were told regretfully that it was not generally available, being compounded to a secret recipe dating back two centuries or more. Well, one meets that kind of thing quite frequently in France . . .

Let me draw a veil over the arrival of the bill, except to mention that after my eyes and the Baron's had met and I'd summed up the situation I let an extra fifty-franc note rest for a moment on the table. The dexterity with which it became forty-two francs twenty reminded me of the skill of a cardsharp. I don't think even the waiter noticed.

Well, he was after all in Guex on the sort of business that doesn't conduce to commonsensical precautions; attending a funeral, I wouldn't think to line my billfold with a wad of spare cash against the chance of going out to dinner with a group of foreign strangers. I let the matter ride. The meal had been superb, and worth far more than we were being charged.

Whether for that reason, though, or because he had found out he was in the company of two writers, or simply because the wines and the liqueur had made him garrulous, he appended to the information he had earlier imparted a few more precise details. His elderly aunt had possessed a *château* nearby (not a castle—the word corresponds quite exactly to the English term "manor house" and need not necessarily have turrets and a moat), and although the lawyers were still wrangling it did seem he must be the closest of her surviving relatives. So he might just, with luck, look forward to inheriting a country seat in keeping with his patent—patent of nobility, that is, a term I'd previously run across only in history books.

By then we were all very mellow, so we toasted his chances in another round of that exquisite liqueur. After which we drove back to Guex.

Carefully.

Arriving at his hotel, we said goodbye in a flurry of alcoholic *bonhomie,* exchanging names and addresses though I don't think we honestly imagined we would meet again, for tomorrow was the last day of the congress, and the Baron had said that directly after the funeral—scheduled for the morning—he was obliged to return to Paris.

But we did in fact cross paths next day. As we were emerging from the cinema after the closing ceremony of the congress, a large black limousine passed which unmistakably belonged to a firm of undertakers. It stopped and backed up, and from its window the Baron called a greeting. With him were three other passengers, all men.

And, although I'd only seen him for as long as it took me and my wife to shake hands with the Baron and confirm our intention of getting in touch again one day, I was certain that one of them was the same who now was bringing in a trolley from the kitchen, on which reposed a dish whose lid when lifted freed into the air the concentrated version of the odour I had already detected in diluted form.

I was instantly detached from the here and now. I had to close my eyes. Never have my nostrils been assailed by so delectable a scent! My mouth watered until I might have drowned in saliva but that all my glands—the very cells of my body!—wanted to experience the aroma and declined to be insulated against it.

When I recovered, more at a loss than ever, I found that something brown and nondescript-looking had been dumped on my plate, which was chipped; that a half-full glass of red wine as sour as the white had been set alongside, while the Baron's water glass had been topped up; and that he was eating busily.

Busily?

This was not the person I had met last year. That version of the Baron not only cared about but loved his food—paid deliberate and sensitive attention to every mouthful of any dish that warranted it. Now he was shovelling the stuff up, apparently determined to clear his plate in record time. And that was absurd. For, as I discovered when I sampled my unprepossessing dollop of what's-it, its flavour matched its aroma. I had taken only a small forkful; nonetheless, as I rolled it across my tongue, choirs sang and flowers burst into bloom and new stars shone in the heavens. I simply did not believe what I was eating.

In the upshot I was reluctant even to swallow that first morsel. I had never dreamed it was possible to create in the modern world a counterpart of ambrosia, the food of the gods. I was afraid to let it slide down my throat for fear the second taste might fall short of the first.

When I did finally get it down in a sort of belated convulsion, I found that the Baron had cleared his plate and was regarding me with a strange expression.

"Ah, you must be enjoying it," he said.

Even as I sought words to express my delight I could feel a tingling warmth moving down me—down not so much in the gravitational as in the evolutionary sense, to lower and lower levels of being, so that instead of just registering on palate and tastebuds and olfactory nerves this stuff, this stew, seemed to be transfusing energy direct into my entire system.

But I did not say so. For I could suddenly read on my host's face what I could also hear unmistakably in his tone of voice: such hopelessness as Mephistopheles might know, something which would be to despair as starvation is to appetite. He spoke as a man who, after long and bitter experience, now knew he would never again enjoy anything.

*   *   *

The tissues of my body were crying out for that miraculous incredible food. I fought and thought for half eternity except that in retrospect I judge it to have been seconds.

And pushed away my plate.

I doubt I shall match that act of will until my dying day. But it was my turn to rise to the occasion, as he had done for stranded foreigners at Guex, and trust to being helped over the consequences.

He stared at me. "Is it possible," he inquired, "that in fact you do not like it?"

"*Mais oui!*" I cried. "I do! But ..." It came to me without warning what I ought to say. "But it's the only food I've tasted in my life which is so delicious that it frightens me."

In one of his books William Burroughs hypothesises a drug to which a person would become addicted after a single dose. I had perhaps had that remark vaguely at the back of my mind. Without having read it, possibly I might not have— Ah, but I had, and I did.

There was a frozen pause. Then a smile spread over the Baron's face so revolutionising in its effect it was like the spring thaw overtaking an arctic landscape.

"I knew I was right," he said. "I knew! If anyone could understand it must be an artist of some kind—an author, a poet ... We shall withdraw so that you may smoke a cigar and I shall instruct Grégoire to bring something to make good the deficiencies of this repast."

He clapped his hands. The servant entered promptly, and stopped dead on seeing my plate practically as full as when he had handed it to me.

"Your dish does not meet with the approval of my guest," the Baron said. "Remove it. Bring fruit and nuts to the *salon.*"

Pushing back my chair, anxious to leave the room, I found the fellow glaring at me. And took stock of him properly for the first time. I cannot say he was ill-favoured; he was of a type one might pass by the thousand on the streets of any city in France. But, as though he had been insulted to his very marrow by my unwillingness to eat what he had prepared, he was regarding me with indescribable malevolence. For a heartbeat or two I could have believed in the Evil Eye.

How had the Baron, a person of taste, hit on this clown for his "gentleman's gentleman"? Was this some hanger-on of his aunt's, tied to him as a condition of her will?

Well, doubtless I should be enlightened soon enough. The time for speculation was over.

As soon as he had recalled Grégoire to his duties, which were sullenly undertaken, the Baron escorted me into the *salon* and from a corner cupboard produced a bottle I thought I recognised. Noticing that I was staring at it, he turned it so that I could read the label. Yes, indeed; it did say *Le Digestif du Tertre*. When he drew the cork and poured me some, I acknowledged the aroma of violets and strawberries and woodruff like an old friend.

The bottle was full; in fact I doubt it had been previously opened. Yet the Baron poured none for himself. Now I could brace myself to ask why.

He answered with the greatest possible obliquity.

"Because," he said, "Grégoire is more than two hundred years old."

I must have looked like a figure in a cartoon film. I had a cigar in one hand and a burning match in the other, and my mouth fell ajar in disbelief and stayed that way until the flame scorched me back to life. Cursing, I disposed of the charred stick and licked my finger.

And was at long last able to say, *"What?"*

"To be precise," the Baron amplified, "he was born in the year the American Revolution broke out, and by the time the French Revolution was launched in imitation of it he was already a turnspit and apprentice *saucier* in the kitchens of my late aunt's *château* near Guex ... which did turn out to devolve on me as her closest surviving relative, but which unfortunately was not accompanied by funds which would have permitted the repair of its neglected fabric. A shame! I found it necessary to realise its value in ready money, and the sum was dismayingly small after the *sacré* lawyer took his share. I said, by the way, my aunt. This is something of a misnomer. According to incontrovertible proofs shown to me by Grégoire, she was my great-aunt at least eleven times over."

I had just had time to visualise a sort of slantwise genealogical tree in which aunts and uncles turned out to be much younger than any of their nephews and nieces, when he corrected himself.

"By that I mean she was my eleven-times-great aunt. Sister of an ancestor on my father's mother's side who was abridged by the guillotine during the Terror, for no fouler crime than having managed his estates better than most of his neighbours and occasionally saved a bit of cash in consequence."

Having made those dogmatic statements, he fixed me with an unwavering gaze and awaited my response.

Was I in two minds? No, I was in half-a-dozen. Out of all the assumptions facing me, the simplest was that the Baron—whom I'd suspected of setting me up for a confidence trick—had himself been brilliantly conned.

Only . . .

By whom? By Grégoire? But in that case he would have carried on with the act when I refused to finish my meal, not scowled as though he wished me to drop dead.

And in addition there was the matter of the food itself. I was having to struggle, even after one brief taste, against the urge to run back and take more, especially since its seductive aroma still permeated the air.

My uncertainty showed on my face. The Baron said, "I can tell that you are not convinced. But I will not weary you by detailing the evidence which has persuaded me. I will not even ask you to credit the argument I put forward—I shall be content if you treat it as one of your fantastic fictions and merely judge whether the plot can be resolved on a happy ending . . . for I swear *I* can't see such an outcome. But already you have proof, do you not? Consult the cells of your body. Are they not reproaching you for eating so little of what was offered?"

Grégoire entered, favouring me with another savage glare, deposited a bowl containing a couple of oranges and some walnuts more or less within reach of me, and went out again. This gave me a chance to bring my chaotic mind under control.

As the door shut, I managed to say, "Who—who invented it?"

The Baron almost crowed with relief, but the sweat pearling on his face indicated how afraid he had been that I would mock him.

"Grégoire's father did," he answered. "A failed alchemist who was driven to accept a post in the kitchens of my family home and there continued his experiments while becoming a renowned *chef*. From Grégoire, though he is a person exceedingly difficult to talk to, I have the impression that his employers believed him to be compounding the Philosophers' Stone and hoped, I imagine, that one day they might find themselves eating off plates of gold that yesterday were pewter ... But he was in fact obsessed with the Elixir of Life, which I confess has always struck me as being by far the most possible of the alchemical goals. Doubtless the succession of delectable dishes which issued from his kitchen and were in part answerable for the decline in my ancestors' fortunes, for such was their fame that the King himself, and many of his relatives and courtiers, used to invite themselves for long stays at our *château*, despite the cramped accommodation it had to offer ... I digress; forgive me.

"As I was about to say, those marvellous dishes were each a step along the path towards his supreme achievement. Ironically, for himself it was too late. Earlier he had been misled into believing that mercury was a sovereign cure for old age, and his frame was so ravaged by ill-judged experiments with it that when he did finally hit on the ideal combination he could only witness its effects on his son, not benefit in person.

"He left his collection of recipes to his son, having previously taught the boy to cook the perfected version by means of such repeated beatings that the child could, and I suspect sometimes did, mix the stuff while half asleep.

"But, possibly because of the mercury poisoning which had made him 'mad as a hatter,' to cite that very apt English phrase, Grégoire *père* overlooked a key point. He omitted to teach the boy how to read and write.

"Finding that his sole bequest from his father was a satchel full of papers, he consulted the only member of the family who had been kind to him: a spinster lady, sister of the then Baron. She did know how to read."

"This is supposed to be the lady you buried just under a year ago?" I demanded.

He gave me a cool look of reproach. "Permit me to lay all before you and reserve your comments . . . ?"

I sighed and nodded and leaned back in my uncomfortable, noisy chair.

"But you are, as it happens, correct," he admitted when he had retrieved the thread of his narrative.

"I cannot show you the satchel I alluded to. Grégoire is keenly aware of its value, though I often suspect he is aware of little else outside his daily cycle from one meal to another. Only because it must have dawned on his loutish brain that he would have to make some adjustment following the death of my—my *aunt*, did he force himself to part with it long enough for me and her lawyer to examine the contents.

"We found inside nearly eighty sheets of paper and five of parchment, all in the same crabbed hand, with what I later established to be a great use of alchemical jargon and an improbably archaic turn of phrase—seventeenth rather than eighteenth century, say the experts I've consulted. How did I get the documents into the hands of experts?

"Well, the lawyer—who is a fool—showed little or no interest in them. He disliked my aunt as you would expect a bigoted peasant to do, inasmuch as since time immemorial it had been known in the district that she lived alone except for a male companion and never put in an appearance at church. Moreover he was furious at having found that in the estate there was only a fraction of the profit he had looked forward to.

"However, he does possess a photocopier, and before Grégoire's terror overcame him to the point of insisting on being given back all his precious papers, I had contrived to feed six or seven of them through the machine. If you're equipped to judge them, I can show them to you. I warn you, though: the language is impenetrably ancient and technical. Have you wondered why my inheritance has not improved my *façon de vivre*? It is upon the attempt to resolve the dilemma posed by Grégoire's patrimony that I've expended what meagre income my portion yields. New clothes, new furniture—such trivia can wait, for if what I believe to be true is true I shall later on have all the time imaginable to make good these transient deficiencies!"

He spoke in the unmistakable tone of someone trying to reassure himself. As much to provide a distraction which would help me not to think about that strange food as for any less selfish reason, I said, "How did Grégoire get his claws into you?"

He laid his finger across his lips with reflex speed. "Do not say such things! Grégoire is the sole repository of a secret which, had it been noised abroad, would have been the downfall of empires!"

Which told me one thing I wanted to know: among the half-dozen papers the Baron had contrived to copy there was *not* the recipe of the dish served to us tonight.

"But your aunt is dead," I countered.

"After more than two hundred years! And I'm convinced she expired thanks to industrial pollution—poisonous organic compounds, heavy metals, disgusting effluents ruining what would otherwise be wholesome foodstuffs . . ."

But his voice tailed away. While he was speaking I had reached for the nuts, cracked one against another in my palm, and was sampling the flesh. There was nothing memorable

about this particular nut, but it was perfectly good, and I found
I could savour it. Moreover I could enjoy the rich smoke of my
cigar. I made it obvious I was doing so—cruelly, perhaps, from
the Baron's point of view, for his eyes hung on my every move-
ment and he kept biting his lower lip. Something, though, made
me feel that my behaviour was therapeutic for him. I rubbed
salt in the wound by topping up my glass of liqueur without
asking permission.

"And in what manner," I inquired, "did your aunt spend her
two centuries of existence? Waiting out a daily cycle from one
meal to the next, always of the same food, as you've said
Grégoire does?"

The Baron slumped.

"I suppose so," he admitted. "At first, with that delirious sensation on one's palate, one thinks, 'Ah, this is the supreme food,
which will never cloy!' After the hundredth day, after the two
hundredth ... Well, you have seen.

"You asked how Grégoire snared me. It was simple—simple
enough for his dull wits to work out a method! How could I decline to share a conveyance, *en route* to and from the funeral,
with my late aunt's sole loyal retainer? How could I decline to
agree when, in the hearing of her lawyer and his *huissier,* he offered to cook me her favourite meal if I would provide him with
the cost of the ingredients? The sum was—well, let me say substantial. Luckily the lawyer, upon whom may there be defeca-
tion, was willing to part with a few *sous* as an advance against
my inheritance.

"And what he gave me was the dish you sampled tonight.
With neither garnishing nor salad nor ... Nothing! He has
never learned to cook anything else, for his father's orders were
explicit: eat this alone, and drink spring water. But he caught
me at my most vulnerable moment. Overwhelmed by the sub-
tlety of the dish, its richness, its fragrance, its ability to arouse
appetite even in a person who, like myself at that time, is given
over to the most melancholy reflections, I was netted like a pi-
geon."

In horrified disbelief I said, "For almost a year you have eaten this same dish over and over, without even a choice of wines to set it off? Without dessert? Without *anything*?"

"But it does work!" he cried. "The longevity of my aunt is evidence! Even though during the Nazi occupation it was hard to find certain important spices, she— Wait! Perhaps it wasn't modern pollution that hastened her end. Perhaps it was lack of those special ingredients while the *sales Boches* were overrunning our beloved country. Perhaps Grégoire kept them back from her, cheated the helpless old lady who had been the only one to help him when he was orphaned!"

"And kept her Elixir to herself, content to watch her brother die, and his wife, and their children and the rest of the family, in the hope of inheriting the lot, which she eventually did. And she then spent her fortune on the food because only Grégoire could tell her how much it was going to cost to buy the necessary ingredients."

The Baron gaped at me. "You talk as if this is all common knowledge," he whispered. I made a dismissive gesture.

"If the recipe works, what other reason can there be for the fact that the rest of her generation aren't still among us?"

"Under the Directory—" he parried.

"If they'd known they had a chance of immortality, it would have made sense for them to realise their assets and bribe their way to safety. You said just now that you will have unimaginable time before you if what you think is actually true. Why didn't the same thought occur to your forebears? Because this old bitch kept the news from them—correct?"

The corners of his mouth turned down. "Truly, life can do no more than imitate art. I invited you to treat this like a plot for a story, and thus far I cannot fault your logic."

"Despite which you plan to imitate someone who shamed not only your family name but indeed her nation and her species?" I crushed my cigar into the nearest ashtray and gulped the rest of my liqueur. "I am appalled! I am revolted! The gastronomic masters of the ages have performed something approaching a miracle. They've transmuted what to savages is mere refuelling into a series of splendid compositions akin to works of art, akin to symphonies, to landscapes, to statues! To leaf through a book like *Larousse Gastronomique* is to find the civilised counterpart of Homer and Vergil—a paean to the heroes who instead of curtailing life amplified it!"

"I think the same—" he began. I cut him short.

"You used to think so, of which I'm well aware. Now you cannot! Now, by your own decision, you've been reduced to the plight of a prisoner who has to coax and wheedle his gaoler before he gets even his daily ration of slop. If a single year has done this to you, what will ten years do, or fifty, or a hundred? What use are you going to make of your oversize lifespan? Do you have plans to reform the world? How appropriate will they be when for decades your mind has been clouded by one solitary obsession?"

I saw he was wavering, and rammed home my advantage.

"And think what you'll be giving up—what you have given up already, on the say-so of a half-moronic turnspit so dull-witted his father couldn't teach him to read! This liqueur, for a start!" I helped myself to more again, and in exaggerated pantomime relished another swig. "Oh, how it brings back that delectable *truite flambée au fenouil* which preceded it, and the marvellous veal, and that salad which on your instructions was dressed as lightly as dewfall . . ."

I am not what they call in French *croyant*. But if there are such things as souls and hells, I think maybe that night I saved one of the former from the latter.

Given my lead, lent reassurance by the way I could see envy gathering in the Baron's face, I waxed lyrical about—making a random choice—oysters *Bercy* and *moules en brochette* and lobster *à l'armoricaine,* invoking some proper wines to correspond. I enthused over quail and partridge and grouse, and from the air I conjured vegetables to serve with them, artichokes and cardoons and salsify and other wonders that the soil affords. These I dressed with sauces so delightfully seasoned I could have sworn their perfume was in the room. I did not, of course, forget that supreme miracle the truffle, nor did I neglect the *cèpe* or the *faux mousseron* or the beefsteak mushroom which is nothing like a steak but gave me *entrée*, as it were, to the main course.

Whereupon I became ecstatic. Roasts and grills, and pies and casseroles and pastries, were succeeded by a roll-call of those cheeses which make walking through a French street-market like entering Aladdin's cave. Then I reviewed fruits of all sizes, shapes, colours, flavours: plums and pomegranates, quinces and medlars, pineapples and nectarines. Then I briefly touched on a few desserts, like *profiteroles* and *crêpes* and *tarte alsacienne* . . .

I was poised to start all over again at the beginning if I must; I had scarcely scraped the surface of even French *cuisine*, and beyond Europe lay China and the Indies and a whole wide world of fabulous fare. But I forbore. I saw suddenly that one shiny drop on the Baron's cheek was not perspiration after all. It was a tear.

Falling silent, I waited.

At length the Baron rose with the air of a man going to face the firing squad. Stiffly, he selected a glass for himself from the tray beside the liqueur bottle, poured himself a slug, and turned to face me, making a half-bow.

"*Mon ami,*" he said with great formality, "I am forever in your debt. Or at any rate, for the duration of my—my *natural* life."

I was afraid he was going to take the drink like medicine, or poison. But instead he checked as he raised it to his lips, inhaled, gave an approving nod, closed his eyes and let a little of it roll around his tongue, smiling.

That was more like it!

He took a second and more generous swig, and resumed his chair.

"That is," he murmured, "a considerable relief. I can after all now appreciate this. I had wondered whether my sense of taste might prove to be negated—whether the food I have subsisted on might entail addiction . . . The latter possibility no doubt remains; however, when all else fails there is always the treatment called *le dindon froid.*"

Or, as they say in English, cold turkey . . . Whatever his other faults, I realised, one could not call the Baron a coward.

"*Ach!*" he went on. "In principle I knew all you have told me months ago. You are right in so many ways, I'm embarrassed by your perspicuity. Am I the person to reform the world? I, whom they have encouraged since childhood to believe that the world's primary function is to provide me with a living regardless of whether or not I have worked to earn it? Sometimes I've been amused to the point of laughing aloud by the silliness of my ambition. And yet—and yet . . .

"*Figurez-vous, mon vieux,* what it is like always to have a voice saying in your head, 'Suppose this time the dish that sustained your aunt two hundred years can be developed into the vehicle of true immortality?' There's no denying that it's a wonderful hybrid between cuisine and medicine."

That I was obliged to grant.

"So, you see, I'm stuck with an appalling moral dilemma," the Baron said. He emptied his glass and set it aside. "It occurs to me," he interpolated, "that I may just have incurred a second one—perhaps infringing Grégoire's father's injunction about eating nothing except his food constitutes a form of suicide? But luckily I feel better for it, so the riddle can be postponed . . . Where was I? Oh, yes: my dilemma. If I break my compact with Grégoire, what's to become of him? If there is no employer to provide him with the funds he needs to buy his ingredients and the kitchen and the pans and stove to cook them, will he die? Or will he be driven like a junkie to robbery and possibly murder? *Mon brave, mon ami,* what the hell am I to do about Grégoire?"

It was as though my panegyric on gastronomy had drained my resources of both speech and enthusiasm. Perhaps more of the liqueur would restore them; I took some.

"By the way," the Baron said, copying me, "an amusing

coincidence! While I was still in Guex-sur-Saône, I recalled . . . Are you all right?"

"I—I think so. Yes," I said.

For a moment I'd been overcome by an irresoluble though fortunately transient problem. I was thinking back on the discourse I'd improvised about cookery when it suddenly dawned on me that I'd praised to the skies things I'd never run across. I hadn't tasted half of what I'd talked about with such excitement, and as for the wines, why, only a millionaire could aspire to keep that lot in his cellar!

This *digestif du Tertre* must be powerful stuff on an empty belly!

Recovering, I said, "Please go on."

"I was about to say that while poring over the papers of Grégoire's that I'd managed to copy, I recalled what the *patron* of the Restaurant du Tertre had said about basing his *digestif* on an eighteenth-century recipe. Thinking that if he had such a recipe he might help me decipher some of those by Grégoire's father, I went back to the restaurant, ostensibly of course to buy a bottle of their speciality—I did in fact buy that very bottle yonder.

"And when, having chatted with the *patron* for a while, I produced the most apposite-seeming of the half-dozen recipes I'd acquired, he was appalled. After scarcely more than a glance, he declared that this was identical with the recipe used for his liqueur, and was on the verge of trying to bribe me and prevent it coming to the notice of a commercial manufacturer!"

Chuckling, he helped himself to half a glassful.

"I mention that not so much as an example of how small-minded people in commerce tend to be—though is it not better that something outstanding should be shared if there is a means of creating enough of it, rather than kept for the private profit of a few?—nor even as a demonstration that the influence of the kitchens at my family's *château* must have lingered long after the declaration of the Republic—no! I cite it as evidence that had he not been obsessed with his alchemical aspirations, Grégoire's father could have become a culinary pioneer to stand beside Carême and Brillat–Savarin, indeed take precedence of them! What a tragedy that his genius was diverted into other channels, and that his son— Well!"

"And yet . . . ." I said.

"And yet . . . ." he echoed, with a heavy sigh.

And that was when I had the only brilliant inspiration of my life.

Or possibly, as I wondered later, credit ought to go to the *digestif.*

At all events, we dined the following night at the Tour d'Argent. And, apart from drinking rather too much so that he wished a hangover on himself, the Baron made an excellent recovery—which removed his last objection to my scheme.

I have one faint regret about the whole affair, and that is that nowadays I have rather less time for my writing. On the other hand I no longer feel the intense financial pressure which so often compelled me to cobble together an unessential bit of made-work simply so that I could meet the bills that month. My routine outgoings are automatically taken care of by the admirable performance of my holdings in Eurobrita Health Food SA, a concern whose product we often patronise and can recommend.

What did we do about Grégoire?

Oh, that was my inspiration. What the Baron had overlooked, you see, was the fact that despite my having slandered him for effect Grégoire was not absolutely stupid. He couldn't be. I confirmed that the moment I put my head around the door of the kitchen he was working in and found it fitted with an electric stove and separate glass-fronted, high-level oven, a far cry from the kitchens at the family *château* with their open fires of wood. A few minutes of questioning, and he opened up like a mussel in a hot pan, as though he had never before been asked about the one thing he really understood: cooking equipment.

Which, given the character I'd deduced for his longest-term employer, was not I suppose very surprising.

It emerged that he had advanced by way of coal-fired, cast-iron ranges, and then gas, and had even had experience of bottled gas and kerosene stoves, and had gone back to wood during hard times. I think once he burned some furniture, but on that point he would not be pinned down.

Well, with his enormous experience of different sorts of kitchen, did he not think it time he was put in charge of a really large one, with staff under him? And what is more, I pressed, we can give you a title!

His sullenness evaporated on the instant. *That* was the ambition he had cherished all his two centuries of life: to be addressed with an honorific. Truly he was a child of the years before the Revolution! His is not quite the sort of title one used to have in those days, of course, but his experience with so many various means of cooking had borne it in on him that there had been certain changes in the world.

And now, in a room larger than the great hall of the *château*, full of vast stainless-steel vats and boilers, to which the necessary ingredients are delivered by the truckload—being much cheaper bought in bulk—Grégoire rejoices in the status of *Contrôleur du Service de Surveillance Qualitative,* and everybody, even the Baron, calls him *Maître.*

He learned almost before he could grow a beard that he must never discuss his longevity with anybody except his employer, so there has been no trouble on that score; his uncertainty in a big city was put down to the fact that he had been isolated near Guex in a small backward village. Inevitably, someone is sooner or later going to notice that on his unvarying diet he doesn't visibly age.

But that will be extremely good for sales.

What Friends Are For

After Tim killed and buried the neighbours' prize terrier the Pattersons took him to the best-reputed—and most expensive—counsellor in the state: Dr Hend.

They spent forty of the fifty minutes they had purchased snapping at each other in the waiting room outside his office, breaking off now and then when a scream or a smashing noise eluded the soundproofing, only to resume more fiercely a moment later.

Eventually Tim was borne out, howling, by a strong male nurse who seemed impervious to being kicked in the belly with all the force an eight-year-old could muster, and the Pattersons were bidden to take his place in Dr Hend's presence. There was no sign of the chaos the boy had caused. The counsellor was a specialist in such cases, and there were smooth procedures for eliminating incidental mess.

"Well, doctor?" Jack Patterson demanded.

Dr Hend studied him thoughtfully for a long moment, then glanced at his wife Lorna, re-confirming the assessment he had made when they arrived. On the male side: expensive clothing, bluff good looks, a carefully constructed image of success. On the female: the most being made of what had to begin with been a somewhat shallow prettiness, even more expensive clothes, plus ultra-fashionable hair style, cosmetics and perfume.

He said at last, "That son of yours is going to be in court very shortly. Even if he is only eight, chronological."

"What?" Jack Patterson erupted. "But we came here to—"

"You came here," the doctor cut in, "to be told the truth. It was your privilege to opt for a condensed-development child. You did it after being informed of the implications. Now you must face up to your responsibilities."

"No, we came here for help!" Lorna burst out. Her husband favoured her with a scowl: *shut up!*

"You have seven minutes of my time left," Dr Hend said wearily. "You can spend it wrangling, or listening to me. Shall I proceed?"

The Pattersons exchanged sour looks, then both nodded.

"*Thank* you. I can see precisely one alternative to having your child placed in a public institution. You'll have to get him a Friend."

"What? And show the world we can't cope?" Jack Patterson rasped. "You must be out of your mind!"

Dr Hend just gazed at him.

"They're—they're terribly expensive, aren't they?" Lorna whispered.

The counsellor leaned back and set his fingertips together.

"As to being out of my mind . . . Well, I'm in good company. It's customary on every inhabited planet we know of to entrust the raising of the young to Friends programmed by a consensus of opinion among other intelligent races. There was an ancient proverb about not seeing the forest for the trees; it is well established that the best possible advice regarding optimum exploitation of juvenile talent comes from those who can analyse the local society in absolute, rather than committed, terms. And the habit is growing commoner here. Many families, if they can afford to, acquire a Friend from choice, not necessity.

"As to expense—yes, Mrs Patterson, you're right. Anything which has had to be shipped over interstellar distances can hardly be cheap. But consider: this dog belonging to your neighbours was a show champion with at least one Best-of-Breed certificate, quite apart from being the boon companion of their small daughter. I imagine the courts will award a substantial sum by way of damages . . . Incidentally, did Tim previously advance the excuse that he couldn't stand the noise it made when it barked?"

"Uh . . ." Jack Patterson licked his lips. "Yes, he did."

"I suspected it might have been rehearsed. It had that kind of flavour. As did his excuse for breaking the arm of the little boy who was the best batter in your local junior ball team, and the excuse for setting fire to the school's free-fall gymnasium, and so forth. You have to accept the fact, I'm afraid, that thanks to his condensed-development therapy your son is a total egocentric. The universe has never yet proved sufficiently intractable to progress him out of the emotional stage most infants leave behind about the time they learn to walk. Physically he is ahead of the average for his age. Emotionally, he is concerned about nothing but his own gratification. He's incapable of empathy, sympathy, worrying about the opinions of others. He is a classic case of arrested personal development."

"But we've done everything we can to—"

"Yes, indeed you have. And it is not enough." Dr Hend allowed the comment to rankle for a few seconds, then resumed.

"We were talking about expense. Well, let me remind you that it costs a lot of money to maintain Tim in the special school you've been compelled to send him to because he made life hell for his classmates at a regular school. The companionship of a Friend is legally equivalent to a formal course of schooling. Maybe you weren't aware of that."

"Sure!" Jack snapped. "But—oh, hell! I simply don't fancy the idea of turning my son over to some ambulating alien artefact!"

"I grant it may seem to you to be a radical step, but juvenile maladjustment is one area where the old saw remains true, about desperate diseases requiring desperate measures. And have you considered the outcome if you don't adopt a radical solution?"

It was clear from their glum faces that they had, but he spelled it out for them nonetheless.

"By opting for a modified child, you rendered yourselves liable for his maintenance and good behaviour for a minimum period of twenty years, regardless of divorce or other legal interventions. If Tim is adjudged socially incorrigible, you will find yourselves obliged to support him indefinitely in a state institution. At present the annual cost of keeping one patient in such an establishment is thirty thousand dollars. Inflation at the current rate will double that by the twenty-year mark, and in view of the extensive alterations you insisted on having made in Tim's heredity I think it unlikely that any court would agree to discontinue your liability as early as twelve years from now. I put it to you that the acquisition of a Friend is your only sensible course of action—whatever you may think of the way alien intelligences have evaluated our society. Besides, you don't have to buy one. You can always rent."

He glanced at his desk clock. "I see your time is up. Good morning. My bill will be faxed to you this afternoon."

That night there was shouting from the living-area of the Patterson house. Tim heard it, lying in bed with the door ajar, and grinned from ear to shell-like ear. He was an extremely beautiful child, with curly fair hair, perfectly proportioned features, ideally regular teeth, eyes blue and deep as mountain pools, a sprinkling of freckles as per specification to make him a trifle less angelic, a fraction more boy-like, and—naturally—big for his age. That had been in the specification, too.

Moreover his vocabulary was enormous compared to an unmodified kid's—as was his IQ, theoretically, though he had never cooperated on a test which might have proved the fact—and he fully understood what was being said.

"You and your goddamned vanity! Insisting on all those special features like wavy golden hair and baby-blue eyes and—and, my God, *freckles!* And now the little devil is apt to drive us into bankruptcy! Have you *seen* what it costs to rent a Friend, even a cheap one from Procyon?"

"Oh, stop trying to lay all the blame on me, will you? They warned you that your demand for tallness and extra strength might be incompatible with the rest, and you took not a blind bit of notice—"

"But he's a boy, dammit, a *boy,* and if you hadn't wanted him to look more like a girl—!"

"I did not, I did not! I wanted him to be *handsome* and you wanted to make him into some kind of crazy beefcake type, loaded down with useless muscles! Just because you never made the college gladiator squad he was condemned before birth to—"

"One more word about what I *didn't* do, and I'll smash your teeth down your ugly throat! How about talking about what I *have* done for a change? Youngest area manager in the corporation, tipped to be the youngest-ever vice-president ... Small thanks to you, of course. When I think where I might have got to by now if you hadn't been tied around my neck—!"

Tim's grin grew so wide it was almost painful. He was becoming drowsy because that outburst in the counsellor's office had expended a lot of energy, but there was one more thing he could do before he dropped off to sleep. He crept from his bed, went to the door on tiptoe, and carefully urinated through the gap on to the landing carpet outside. Then, chuckling, he scrambled back under the coverlet and a few minutes later was lost in colourful dreams.

The doorbell rang when his mother was in the bathroom and his father was calling on the lawyers to see whether the matter of the dog could be kept out of court after all.

At once Lorna yelled, "Tim, stay right where you are—I'll get it!"

But he was already heading for the door at a dead run. He liked being the first to greet a visitor. It was such fun to show himself stark naked and shock puritanical callers, or scream and yell about how Dad had beaten him mercilessly, showing off bruises collected by banging into furniture and blood trickling from cuts and scratches. But today an even more inspired idea came to him, and he made a rapid detour through the kitchen and raided the garbage pail as he passed.

He opened the door with his left hand and delivered a soggy mass of rotten fruit, vegetable peelings and coffee grounds with his right, as hard as he could and at about face-height for a grownup.

Approximately half a second later the whole loathsome mass splattered over him, part on his face so that his open mouth tasted the foulness of it, part on his chest so that it dropped inside his unzipped shirt. And a reproachful voice said, "Tim! I'm your Friend! And that's no way to treat a friend, is it?"

Reflex had brought him to the point of screaming. His lungs were filling, his muscles were tensing, when he saw what had arrived on the threshold and his embryo yell turned into a simple gape of astonishment.

The Friend was humanoid, a few inches taller than himself and a great deal broader, possessed of two legs and two arms and a head with eyes and a mouth and a pair of ears ... but it was covered all over in shaggy fur of a brilliant emerald green. Its sole decoration—apart from a trace of the multi-coloured garbage it had caught and heaved back at him which still adhered to the palm of its left hand—was a belt around its waist bearing a label stamped in bright red letters AUTHORISED AUTONOMIC ARTEFACT (SELF-DELIVERING), followed by the Patterson family's address.

"Invite me in," said the apparition. "You don't keep a friend standing on the doorstep, you know, and I am your Friend, as I just explained."

"Tim! *Tim!*" At a stumbling run, belting a robe around her, his mother appeared from the direction of the bathroom, a towel clumsily knotted over her newly-washed hair. On seeing the nature of the visitor, she stopped dead.

"But the rental agency said not to expect you until—" She broke off. It was the first time in her life she had spoken to an alien biofact, although she had seen many both live and on trivee.

"We were able to include more than the anticipated quantity in the last shipment from Procyon," the Friend said. "There has been an advance in packaging methods. Permit me to identify myself." It marched past Tim and removed its belt, complete with label, and handed it to Lorna. "I trust you will find that I conform to your requirements."

"You stinking bugger! I won't have you fucking around in my home!" Tim shrieked. He had small conception of what the words he was using meant, except in a very abstract way, but he was sure of one thing: they always made his parents good and mad.

The Friend, not sparing him a glance, said, "Tim, you should have introduced me to your mother. Since you did not I am having to introduce myself. Do not compound your impoliteness by interrupting, because that makes an even worse impression."

"Get out!" Tim bellowed, and launched himself at the Friend in a flurry of kicking feet and clenched fists. At once he found himself suspended a foot off the floor with the waistband of his pants tight in a grip like a crane's.

To Lorna the Friend said, "All you're requested to do is thumbprint the acceptance box and fax the datum back to the rental company. That is, if you do agree to accept me."

She looked at it, and her son, for a long moment, and then firmly planted her thumb on the reverse of the label.

"Thank you. Now, Tim!" The Friend swivelled him around so that it could look directly at him. "I'm sorry to see how dirty you are. It's not the way one would wish to find a friend. I shall give you a bath and a change of clothes."

"I had a bath!" Tim howled, flailing arms and legs impotently.

Ignoring him, the Friend continued, "Mrs Patterson, if you'll kindly show me where Tim's clothes are kept, I'll attend to the matter right away."

A slow smile spread over Lorna's face. "You know something?" she said to the air. "I guess that counsellor was on the right track after all. Come this way—uh . . . Say! What do we call you?"

"It's customary to have the young person I'm assigned to select a name for me."

"If I know Tim," Lorna said, "he'll pick on something so filthy it can't be used in company!"

Tim stopped screaming for a moment. That was an idea which hadn't occurred to him.

"But," Lorna declared, "we'll avoid that, and just call you Buddy right from the start. Is that okay?"

"I shall memorise the datum at once. Come along, Tim!"

"Well, I guess it's good to find such prompt service these days," Jack Patterson muttered, looking at the green form of Buddy curled up by the door of Tim's bedroom. Howls, yells and moans were pouring from the room, but during the past half-hour they had grown less loud, and sometimes intervals of two or three minutes interrupted the racket, as though exhaustion were overcoming the boy. "I still hate to think what the neighbours are going to say, though. It's about the most public admission of defeat that parents can make, to let their kid be seen with one of those things at his heels!"

"Stop thinking about what the neighbours will say and think about how I feel for once!" rapped his wife. "You had an easy day today—"

"The hell I did! Those damned lawyers—!"

"You were sitting in a nice quiet office! If it hadn't been for Buddy, I'd have had more than even my usual kind of hell! I think Dr Hend had a terrific idea. I'm impressed."

"Typical!" Jack grunted. "You can't cope with this, buy a machine, you can't cope with that, buy another machine ... Now it turns out you can't even cope with your own son. *I'm* not impressed!"

"Why, you goddamned—!"

"Look, I paid good money to make sure of having a kid who'd be bright and talented and a regular all-around guy, and I got one. But who's been looking after him? You have! You've screwed him up with your laziness and bad temper!"

"How much time do *you* waste on helping to raise him?" She confronted him, hands on hips and eyes aflame. "Every evening it's the same story, every weekend it's the same—'get this kid off my neck because I'm worn out!' "

"Oh, shut up. It sounds as though he's finally dropped off. Want to wake him again and make things worse? I'm going to fix a drink. I need one."

He spun on his heel and headed downstairs. Fuming, Lorna followed him.

By the door of Tim's room, Buddy remained immobile except that one of his large green ears swivelled slightly and curled over at the tip.

At breakfast next day Lorna served hot cereal—to Buddy as well as Tim, because among the advantages of this model of Friend was the fact that it could eat anything its assigned family was eating.

Tim picked up his dish as soon as it was set before him and threw it with all his might at Buddy. The Friend caught it with such dexterity that hardly a drop splashed on the table.

"Thank you, Tim," it said, and ate the lot in a single slurping mouthful. "According to my instructions you like this kind of cereal, so giving it to me is a very generous act. Though you might have delivered the dish somewhat more gently."

Tim's semi-angelic face crumpled like a mask made of wet paper. He drew a deep breath, and then flung himself forward across the table, aiming to knock everything off it on to the floor. Nothing could break—long and bitter experience had taught the Pattersons to buy only resilient plastic utensils—but spilling the milk, sugar, juice and other items could have made a magnificent mess.

A hair's breadth away from the nearest object, the milk-jug, Tim found himself pinioned in a gentle but inflexible clutch.

"It appears that it is time to begin lessons for the day," Buddy said. "Excuse me, Mrs Patterson. I shall take Tim into the back yard where there is more space."

"To begin lessons?" Lorna echoed. "Well—uh ... But he hasn't had any breakfast yet!"

"If you'll forgive my saying so, he has. He chose not to eat it. He is somewhat overweight, and one presumes that lunch will be served at the customary time. Between now and noon it is unlikely that malnutrition will claim him. Besides, this offers an admirable opportunity for a practical demonstration of the nature of mass, inertia and friction."

With no further comment Buddy rose and, carrying Tim in effortless fashion, marched over to the door giving access to the yard.

"So how has that hideous green beast behaved today?" Jack demanded.

"Oh, it's fantastic! I'm starting to get the hang of what it's designed to do." Lorna leaned back in her easy chair with a smug expression.

"Yes?" Jack's face by contrast was sour. "Such as what?"

"Well, it puts up with everything Tim can do—and that's a tough job because he's pulling out all the stops he can think of—and interprets it in the most favourable way it can. It keeps insisting that it's Tim's Friend, so he's doing what a friend ought to do."

Jack blinked at her. "What the hell are you talking about?" he rasped.

"If you'd listen, you might find out!" she snapped back. "He threw his breakfast at Buddy, so Buddy ate it and said thank you. Then because he got hungry he climbed up and got at the candy jar, and Buddy took that and ate the lot and said thank you again, and ... Oh, it's all part of a pattern, and very clever."

"Are you crazy? You let this monstrosity eat not only Tim's breakfast but all his candy, and you didn't try and stop it?"

"I don't think you read the instructions," Lorna said.

"Quit needling me, will you? Of course I read the instructions!"

"Then you know that if you interfere with what a Friend

does, your contract is automatically void and you have to pay the balance of the rental in a lump sum!"

"And how is it interfering to give your own son some more breakfast in place of what the horrible thing took?"

"But Tim threw his dish at—!"

"If you gave him a decent diet he'd—!"

It continued. Above, on the landing outside Tim's door, Buddy kept his furry green ears cocked, soaking up every word.

"Tim!"

"Shut up, you fucking awful nuisance!"

"Tim, if you climb that tree past the first fork, you will be on a branch that's not strong enough to bear your weight. You will fall about nine feet to the ground, and the ground is hard because the weather this summer has been so dry."

"*Shut up!* All I want is to get away from you!"

Crack!

"What you are suffering from is a bruise, technically called a subcutaneous haemorrhage. That means a leak of blood under the skin. You also appear to have a slight rupture of the left Achilles tendon. That's this sinew here, which . . ."

"In view of your limited skill in swimming, it's not advisable to go more than five feet from the edge of this pool. Beyond that point the bottom dips very sharply."

"*Shut up!* I'm trying to get away from you, so—*glug!*"

"Insufficient oxygen is dissolved in water to support an air-breathing creature like a human. Fish, on the other hand, can utilise the oxygen dissolved in water, because they have gills and not lungs. Your ancestors . . ."

"Why, there's that little bastard Tim Patterson! And look at what he's got trailing behind him! Hey, Tim! Who said you had to live with this funny green teddy bear? Did you have to go have your head shrunk?"

Crowding around him, a dozen neighbourhood kids, both sexes, various ages from nine to fourteen.

"Tim's head as you can doubtless see is of normal proportions. I am assigned to him as his Friend."

"Hah! Don't give us that shit! Who'd want to be a friend of Tim's? He busted my brother's arm and laughed about it!"

"He set fire to the gym at my school!"

"He killed my dog—he killed my Towser!"

"So I understand. Tim, you have the opportunity to say you were sorry, don't you?"

"Ah, he made that stinking row all the time, barking his silly head off—"

"You bastard! *You killed my dog!*"

"Buddy, help! *Help!*"

"As I said, Tim, you have an excellent opportunity to say how sorry you are ... No, little girl: please put down that rock. It's extremely uncivil, and also dangerous, to throw things like that at people."

"Shut up!"

"Let's beat the hell out of him! Let him go whining back home and tell how all those terrible kids attacked him, and see how he likes his own medicine!"

"Kindly refrain from attempting to inflict injuries on my assigned charge."

"I told you to shut up, greenie!"

"I did caution you, as you'll recall. I did say that it was both uncivil and dangerous to throw rocks at people. I believe what I should do is inform your parents. Come, Tim."

"No!"

"Very well, as you wish. I shall release this juvenile to continue the aggression with rocks."

"No!"

"But, Tim, your two decisions are incompatible. Either you come with me to inform this child's parents of the fact that rocks were thrown at you, or I shall have to let go and a great many more rocks will probably be thrown—perhaps more than I can catch before they hit you."

"I—uh . . . I—I'm sorry that I hurt your dog. It just made me so mad that he kept on barking and barking all the time, and never shut up!"

"But he didn't bark all the time! He got hurt—he cut his paw and he wanted help!"

"He did *so* bark all the time!"

"He did not! You just got mad because he did it that one time!"

"I—uh . . . Well, I guess maybe . . ."

"To be precise, there had been three complaints recorded about your dog's excessive noise. On each occasion you had gone out and left him alone for several hours."

"Right! Thank you, Buddy! *See?*"

"But you didn't have to kill him!"

"Correct, Tim. You did not. You could have become acquainted with him, and then looked after him when it was necessary to leave him by himself."

"Ah, who'd want to care for a dog like that shaggy brute?"

"Perhaps someone who never was allowed his own dog?"

"Okay. *Okay!* Sure I wanted a dog, and they never let me have one! Kept saying I'd—I'd torture it or something! So I said fine, if that's how you think of me, let's go right ahead! You always like to be proven right!"

"Kind of quiet around here tonight," Jack Patterson said. "What's been going on?"

"You can thank Buddy," Lorna answered.

"Can I now? So what's he done that I can't do, this time?"

"Persuaded Tim to go to bed on time and without yelling his head off, that's what!"

"Don't feed me that line! 'Persuaded!' Cowed him, don't you mean?"

"All I can say is that tonight's the first time he's let Buddy sleep inside the room instead of on the landing by the door."

"You keep saying I didn't read the instructions—now it turns out *you* didn't read them! Friends don't sleep, not the way we do at any rate. They're supposed to be on watch twenty-four hours per day."

"Oh, stop it! The first peaceful evening we've had in heaven knows how long, and you're determined to ruin it!"

"I am not!"

"Then why the hell don't you keep quiet?"

Upstairs, beyond the door of Tim's room which was as ever ajar, Buddy's ears remained alert with their tips curled over to make them acoustically ultra-sensitive.

"Who—? Oh! I know *you!* You're Tim Patterson, aren't you? Well, what do you want?"

"I . . . I . . ."

"Tim wishes to know whether your son would care to play ball with him, madam."

"You have to be joking! I'm not going to let Teddy play with Tim after the way Tim broke his elbow with a baseball bat!"

"It did happen quite a long time ago, madam, and—"

"No! That's final! *No!*"

Slam!

"Well, thanks for trying, Buddy. It would have been kind of fun to . . . Ah, well!"

"That little girl is ill-advised to play so close to a road carrying fast traffic— Oh, dear. Tim, I shall need help in coping with this emergency. Kindly take off your belt and place it around her leg about *here* . . . That's correct. Now pull it tight. See how the flow of blood is reduced? You've put a tourniquet on the relevant pressure point, that's to say a spot where a large artery passes near the skin. If much blood were allowed to leak, it might be fatal. I note there is a pen in the pocket of her dress. Please write a letter T on her forehead, and add the exact time; you see there's a clock over there. When she gets to the hospital the surgeon will know how long the blood-supply to her leg has been cut off. It must not be restricted more than twenty minutes."

"Uh ... Buddy, I can't write a T. And I can't tell the time either."

"How old did you say you were?"

"Well ... Eight. And a half."

"Yes, Tim. I'm actually aware both of your age and of your incompetence. Give me the pen, please ... There. Now go to the nearest house and ask someone to telephone for an ambulance. Unless the driver, who I see is backing up, has a phone right in his car."

"Yes, what do you want?" Jack Patterson stared at the couple who had arrived without warning on the doorstep.

"Mr Patterson? I'm William Vickers, from up on the 1100 block, and this is my wife Judy. We thought we ought to call around after what your boy Tim did today. Louise—that's our daughter—she's still in the hospital, of course, but ... Well, they say she's going to make a quick recovery."

"What the hell is that about Tim?" From the living-area Lorna emerged, glowering and reeking of gin. "Did you say Tim put your daughter in the hospital? Well, that finishes it! Jack Patterson, I'm damned if I'm going to waste any more of my life looking after your goddamned son! I am through with him and you both—d'you hear me? *Through!*"

"But you've got it all wrong," Vickers protested feebly. "Thanks to his quick thinking, and that Friend who goes with him everywhere, Louise got off amazingly lightly. Just some cuts, and a bit of blood lost—nothing serious. Nothing like as badly hurt as you'd expect a kid to be when a car had knocked her down."

Lorna's mouth stood half-open like that of a stranded fish. There was a pause; then Judy Vickers plucked at her husband's sleeve.

"Darling, I—uh—think we came at a bad moment. We ought to get on home. But . . . Well, you do understand how grateful we are, don't you?"

She turned away, and so, after a bewildered glance at both Jack and Lorna, did her husband.

"You stupid bitch!" Jack roared. "Why the hell did you have to jump to such an idiotic conclusion? Two people come around to say thanks to Tim for—for whatever the hell he did, and *you* have to assume the worst! Don't you have any respect for your son at all . . . or any love?"

"Of course I love him! I'm his mother! I do care about him!" Lorna was returning to the living-area, crabwise because her head was turned to shout at Jack over her shoulder. "For you, though, he's nothing but a possession, a status symbol, a—"

"A correction, Mrs Patterson," a firm voice said. She gasped and whirled. In the middle of the living-area's largest rug was Buddy, his green fur making a hideous clash with the royal blue of the oblong he was standing on.

"Hey! What are you doing down here?" Jack exploded. "You're supposed to be up with Tim!"

"Tim is fast asleep and will remain so for the time being," the Friend said calmly. "Though I would suggest that you keep your voices quiet."

"Now look here! I'm not going to take orders from—"

"Mr Patterson, there is no question of orders involved. I simply wish to clarify a misconception on your wife's part. While she has accurately diagnosed your attitude towards your son— as she just stated, you have never regarded him as a person, but only as an attribute to bolster your own total image which is that of the successful corporation executive—she is still under the misapprehension that she, quotes on and off, 'loves' Tim. It would be more accurate to say that she welcomes his intractability because it offers her the chance to vent her jealousy against you. She resents— No, Mrs Patterson, I would not recommend the employment of physical violence. I am engineered to a far more rapid level of nervous response than human beings enjoy."

One arm upraised, with a heavy cut-crystal glass in it poised ready to throw, Lorna hesitated, then sighed and repented.

"Yeah, okay. I've seen you catch everything Tim's thrown at you . . . But you shut up, hear me?" With a return of her former rage. "It's no damned business of yours to criticise me! Nor Jack either!"

"Right!" Jack said. "I've never been so insulted in my life!"

"Perhaps it would have been salutary for you to be told some unpleasant truths long ago," Buddy said. "My assignment is to help actualise the potential which—I must remind you—you arranged to build into Tim's genetic endowment. He did not ask to be born the way he is. He did not ask to come into the world as the son of parents who were so vain they could not be content with a natural child, but demanded the latest luxury model. You have systematically wasted his talents. No child of eight years and six months with an IQ in the range 160–175 should be incapable of reading, writing, telling the time, counting and so forth. This is the predicament you've wished on Tim."

"If you don't shut up I'll—!"

"Mr Patterson, I repeat my advice to keep your voice down."

"I'm not going to take advice or any other kind of nonsense from you, you green horror!"

"Nor am I!" Lorna shouted. "To be told I don't love my own son, and just use him as a stick to beat Jack with—"

"Right, *right!* And I'm not going to put up with being told I treat him as some kind of ornament, a . . . What did you call it?"

Prompt, Buddy said, "An attribute to bolster your image."

"That's it— Now just a second!" Jack strode towards the Friend. "You're making mock of me, aren't you?"

"And me!" Lorna cried.

"Well, I've had enough! First thing tomorrow morning I call the rental company and tell them to take you away. I'm sick of having you run our lives as though we were morons unfit to look after ourselves, and above all I'm sick of my son being put in charge of— Tim! What the hell are you doing out of bed?"

"I did advise you to speak more quietly," Buddy murmured.

"Get back to your room at once!" Lorna stormed at the small tousle-haired figure descending the stairs in blue pyjamas. Tears were streaming across his cheeks, glistening in the light of the living-area's lamps.

"Didn't you hear your mother?" Jack bellowed. "Get back to bed this minute!"

But Tim kept on coming down, with stolid determined paces, and reached the floor-level and walked straight towards Buddy and linked his thin pink fingers with Buddy's green furry ones. Only then did he speak.

"You're not going to send Buddy away! This is my Friend!"

"Don't use that tone to your father! I'll do what the hell I like with that thing!"

"No, you won't." Tim's words were full of finality. "You aren't allowed to. I read the contract. It says you can't."

"What do you mean, you 'read the contract'?" Lorna rasped. "You can't read anything, you little fool!"

"As a matter of fact, he can," Buddy said mildly. "I taught him to read this afternoon."

"You—you what?"

"I taught him to read this afternoon. The skill was present in his mind but had been rendered artificially latent, a problem which I have now rectified. Apart from certain inconsistent sound-to-symbol relationships, Tim should be capable of reading literally anything in a couple of days."

"And I did so read the contract!" Tim declared. "So I know Buddy can be with me for ever and ever!"

"You exaggerate," Buddy murmured.

"Oh, sure I do! But ten full years is a long time." Tim tightened his grip on Buddy's hand. "So let's not have any more silly talk, hm? And no more shouting either, please. Buddy has explained why kids my age need plenty of sleep, and I guess I ought to go back to bed. Coming, Buddy?"

"Yes, of course. Good night, Mr Patterson—Mrs Patterson. Do please ponder my remarks. And Tim's too, because he knows you so much better than I do."

Turning towards the stairs, Buddy at his side, Tim glanced back with a grave face on which the tears by now had dried.

"Don't worry," he said. "I'm not going to be such a handful any more. I realise now you can't help how you behave."

"He's so goddamned patronising!" Jack Patterson exploded next time he and Lorna were in Dr Hend's office. As part of the out-of-court settlement of the dead dog affair they were obliged to bring Tim here once a month. It was marginally cheaper than hiring the kind of legal computer capacity which might save the kid from being institutionalised.

"Yes, I can well imagine that he must be," Dr Hend sighed. "But, you see, a biofact like Buddy is designed to maximise the characteristics which leading anthropologists from Procyon, Regulus, Sigma Draconis and elsewhere have diagnosed as being beneficial in human society but in dangerously short supply. Chief among these, of course, is empathy. Fellow-feeling, compassion, that kind of thing. And to encourage the development of it, one must start by inculcating patience. Which involves setting an example."

"Patience? There's nothing patient about Tim!" Lorna retorted. "Granted, he used to be self-willed and destructive and foul-mouthed, and that's over, but now he never gives us a moment's peace! All the time it's gimme this, gimme that, I want to make a boat, I want to build a model starship, I want glass so I can make a what's-it to watch ants breeding in ... I want, I want! It's just as bad and maybe worse."

"Right!" Jack said morosely. "What Buddy's done is turn our son against us."

"On the contrary. It's turned him *for* you. However belatedly, he's now doing his best to live up to the ideals you envisaged in the first place. You wanted a child with a lively mind and a high IQ. You've got one." Dr Hend's voice betrayed the fact that his temper was fraying. "He's back in a regular school, he's establishing a fine scholastic record, he's doing well at free-fall gymnastics and medicare and countless other subjects. Buddy has made him over into precisely the sort of son you originally ordered."

"No, I told you!" Jack barked. "He—he kind of looks down on us, and I can't stand it!"

"Mr Patterson, if you stopped to think occasionally you might realise why that could not have been avoided."

"I say it could and should have been avoided!"

"It could not! To break Tim out of his isolation in the shortest possible time, to cure him of his inability to relate to other people's feelings, Buddy used the most practical means at hand. It taught Tim a sense of pity—a trick I often wish I could work, but I'm only human, myself. It wasn't Buddy's fault, any more than it was Tim's, that the first people the boy learned how to pity had to be you.

"So if you want him to switch over to respecting you, you'd better ask Buddy's advice. It'll explain how to go about it. After all, that's what Friends are for: to make us better at being human.

"Now you must excuse me, because I have other clients waiting. Good afternoon!"

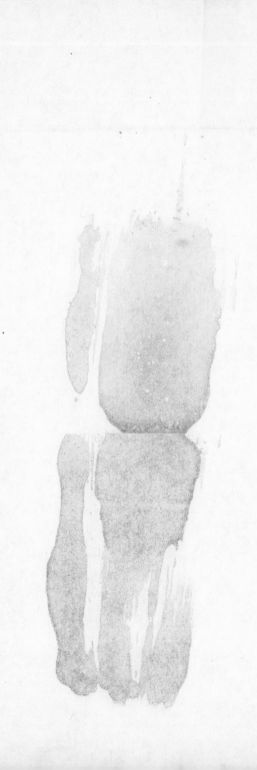